Tomorrow Belongs to Us

Romance Novel on RMS Titanic

Lynda Dunwell

Romantic Reads Publishing

www.RomanticReadsPublishing.com

...

Author's Note:

Due to the nature of the varied reports of the
Titanic disaster, I have taken liberties and filled in
gaps where necessary. Some characters and events
have been fictionalized. I hope the historians
among you will forgive me.

ISBN: 978-1-910712-04-7
Published in the United Kingdom

Cover Design: Selfpubbookcovers/ineedabookcover

Chapter One

London, Spring 1912

Engrossed in the first edition of the *Express*, Lucy Mainwaring thought she was alone in the hall of her uncle's town house. Since she had begun staying with the Grants as companion to her cousin, she had slipped downstairs each morning to read the newspapers. Today she was enjoying an article about the world's largest passenger liner, the *RMS Titanic*. As her aunt, Lady Grant, did not approve of young ladies filling their heads with the contents of the broadsheets, Lucy felt obliged to indulge her passion for the latest news before the family arose.

Somewhere from beyond a sea of newsprint, she heard a man cough. Slowly she looked up and half-expected to see a servant trying to attract her attention. Instead, a tall naval officer stood before her. Surprised by the stranger's appearance, she stepped back and the newspaper slipped out of her hands onto the tiled floor. Embarrassed, she crouched to retrieve the news sheets, but as she stretched forward, she lost her balance and found herself on all fours. "Oh, dear!"

The officer dropped to one knee, gathered up the sheets, and folded the newspaper under his arm. "My most humble apologies, Miss Grant, I didn't mean to startle you. Lieutenant Commander Edwin Hardie, at your service." He offered her his hand.

Lucy went to take it, but froze as their eyes locked. She tried to open her mouth to reply, but no words came out. She felt as though time had been suspended.

"Forgive me," he said, "but Sir Leyster must see all the newspapers immediately."

Lucy's lips warmed to a smile as his voice caressed her like velvet.

"Hardie! What's so damned urgent at this early hour?" bellowed Sir Leyster as he hurried downstairs towards them. He stopped abruptly, halfway down. "What in heaven's name are you doing on the floor?"

Ashamed to be discovered so, Lucy stared at her uncle and stood up. She desperately wanted to explain herself, but what could she say? That she enjoyed reading newspapers, but Lady Grant thought it unseemly for a young lady? That she read the first editions secretly each morning before the master of the house? And today she had been caught in the act by the handsome naval officer standing beside her. "Looking...at the..."

"Newspapers." Hardie finished the sentence for her and indicated the troublesome edition under his arm.

"Looking, eh?" Sir Leyster's face creased as he reached the bottom of the stairs. "Must be country living. In my day, young girls never saw the light of day before noon. Keep a sharp lookout, Hardie, you know what's said about the early bird. Now, follow me!"

Uncertain what to do next, Lucy stood her ground. Were her burning cheeks due to being discovered reading the newspaper, grovelling on the floor, or not correcting Hardie's initial mistake in confusing her with her cousin? She didn't know, but there was no time for explanations.

Hardie collected the remainder of the morning editions from the hall table and followed his superior. The study door closed behind them with a thud that brought Lucy back to reality. The heat of yet another blush swept over her as she ran her finger around her high-necked collar and tried to cool her face with the back of her hand.

Back in her bedroom she paced the floor, unable to get Lieutenant-Commander Hardie out of her mind. But how could he have confused her with Cecilly? They were cousins, but there was little resemblance. Cecilly favoured her mother, blonde and blue-eyed. Lucy had auburn hair and brown eyes. *I'm taller and five years older; I should be wiser!*

* * * *

"This had better be important, Hardie. When you were appointed to my office I thought I made it perfectly clear that I was not to be disturbed at home."

"Indeed, sir, but I was ordered to deliver this message to you immediately." He handed the sealed envelope to his superior. "Several of today's broadsheets carry similar stories which you must see, sir." Hardie spread the Fleet Street first editions out on the desk.

Sir Leyster broke the Admiralty seal and paused to read the contents. When he finished, he scanned the open news sheets for a few moments before looking up. "What do I need to know that's not covered by these stories?"

Quickly Hardie outlined the escalating spate of thefts of highly sensitive naval and military documents throughout Europe. "Now it's started in London. I understand, sir, you will be briefed on which plans have been stolen later this morning by the Home Secretary. There appears to be no immunity. Of course, everyone's denying they are victims. But evidence indicates a major spy ring in operation. Using a network of agents, sensitive information is being stolen, and military secrets are auctioned off to the highest bidder."

Sir Leyster raised his bushy eyebrows. "Have we no idea who's behind this?"

Hardie shook his head. "It has to be someone who can move freely around Europe and is known in the most intimate circles. He—or they, for I doubt he works alone—must enjoy the protection of at least one European power."

"European? Are you certain there's no American involvement?"

"Nothing to indicate so at present, but with President Taft supporting isolationism, you know how inward looking American foreign policy can be."

Sir Leyster nodded. "Ironic, isn't it? The Americans claim to want nothing to do with European affairs yet come flocking to the Continent once they've made their fortunes. Doubtless the town will be overflowing with them again once the Season gets underway. Why, even my own daughter claims to have lost her heart to a young Yankee."

Hardie found Sir Leyster's last remark cut more deeply than he would have expected. The attractive young woman he had just met in the hall was in love with an American. "I trust the young man is an early bird too."

"Early bird? Whatever do you mean?"

"Your daughter, sir. Outside in the hall a few minutes ago, you called her an early bird."

"Really?" Sir Leyster chuckled.

Feeling awkward, Hardie shifted his weight from one foot to the other and back. "Please accept my apology. I wouldn't have been so forward with the young lady had I been aware of the circumstances."

"Are you saying your early morning liaison was pre-arranged?"

"Definitely not, sir! Upon my word, our meeting was accidental. This is the first time I have visited your home. Now I know the lady is no longer free, I assure you there will be no further meetings."

"What a pity." He rose to his feet. "Hardie, you have my permission to talk to the girl as often as you like, providing your intentions are honourable."

"But, sir, you implied your daughter's affections were engaged elsewhere."

"Aye, so I'm led to believe, but I was speaking of Cecilly, who would never be abroad at this early hour. The lady you took obvious pleasure in meeting this morning is my niece, Lucy Mainwaring. She is my late sister's daughter and is staying with us for a while."

* * * *

"What are you wearing tomorrow night?" Cecilly asked, lounging on Lucy's bed.

"I have my cream silk. Do you remember it? I wore it at your coming-out."

"But this is an embassy ball!"

"I've not worn it since," Lucy claimed, hoping the gown's lack of use might give her younger companion some consolation.

"Haven't you been to a ball since last summer? You poor thing! Whatever can your father be thinking of, shutting you away all the time?"

"I am not *shut away*. Life at the rectory is parochial."

"Don't you mean boring?"

"We attend many local functions, but it would be quite wrong for me, as the rector's daughter, to out dress all the other ladies."

"Serves them right for being so dowdy."

"But I won't be *dowdy* in my cream silk tomorrow night, will I?"

"No, just out of fashion." Cecilly dangled her legs over the side of the bed. "Important people will be there, and it *matters* what a lady wears in London."

Lucy's face creased with concern. "Is that all you've learned since you came out?"

"Of course it isn't." Cecilly jumped to her feet. "I've got a brilliant idea. You can wear one of mine."

"I'm taller than you."

"It won't matter."

"I've already decided on the cream."

Cecilly pouted. "Stubborn as ever. Will nothing ever change you?"

Lucy gave her a knowing look in reply.

"It will be your downfall. Men don't like stubborn women." Cecilly placed her hands firmly on her hips. "Mama says so."

And she should know, thought Lucy.

"At least try on some of my gowns," Cecilly said. "I'll get Monique to pick out a few. She's so skilled with a needle she could alter a gown for you in next to no time. You can try them on when we get back from Dorchester House."

Later that afternoon, Lady Grant, Cecilly, and Lucy journeyed in the motor car to Dorchester House to attend an afternoon reception hosted by the American ambassador's wife, Mrs. Reid. As they entered Park Lane, Lady Grant said, "Lucy, my dear, we really must do something about getting you settled. I would be failing in my duty as your aunt if I didn't help with a few introductions. I'll see what I can do."

Lucy found the whole idea repugnant and wanted desperately to object to any matchmaking activities on her behalf. However, as a guest in the Grant's house, it wasn't her place to speak out so boldly.

"Your father's brains must be addled," her ladyship declared, "burying you in the country without a thought for your marital prospects. I suppose he intends to keep you at home?"

"I think—"

"Leave thinking to the gentlemen. A young lady must marry. I'm sure your dear mother, God rest her soul, would have agreed with me. Mary wouldn't have allowed *your* best years to be frittered away in the country. She had good sense, which is more than I can say of your father, although I should not speak ill of a man of the cloth. He should never have allowed you to become a governess in France. The least said of that, the better!"

Lucy flinched at her aunt's words. Mary Mainwaring had died twelve years previously. Lucy had filled her teenage years with extensive reading. By the time she was Cecilly's age, she had read so many romantic novels she had believed she would fall in love and then marry. It hadn't happened. Now at twenty-three, she recognised that possession of a sizable dowry provided any woman, regardless of age, with admirers. Hence with no fortune, a lack of suitors, and her father's permission, Lucy had become a governess. And she would probably be seeking employment again when she left the Grants.

As they drew up at the entrance to Dorchester House, Lucy looked up in awe at the building.

"It's even more impressive inside," Cecily said.

"The Reids are well known for the lavish functions they have hosted in recent years," Lady Grant added. "The wedding reception for their daughter a few years ago was very memorable. It was the talk of the town for the entire Season."

Inwardly Lucy breathed a sigh of relief that Lady Grant had been distracted from matchmaking plans. The popularity of the Reids as society hosts did not interest her, but she was eager to see the interior of the house she had read so much about in the newspapers.

After they had been announced and greeted by the ambassador's wife, Lady Grant turned to the girls. "Stay here, keep together, and don't speak to anyone you haven't been introduced to. I've just seen a friend of mine and I must have a word with her."

Lucy watched her aunt glide between various groups of people. She saw men clad in military and diplomatic uniforms, and ladies dressed in pale-coloured lace gowns with large, matching hats. When Lady Grant reached an elderly matron dressed from head to toe in lavender she halted, and their greeting appeared to be one of warm affection.

Content to stand and breathe in the ambiance, Lucy watched the elegant saloon rapidly fill with guests. As more people arrived, the room throbbed with conversation, and somewhere in the background a string quartet played.

Cecilly leaned close to her cousin. "Mother persists in asking questions about Frank's family. I'm sure she is talking about him now, checking on his eligibility and standing in American society."

"I think you are letting your imagination run away with you, cousin. Surely that has been looked into most carefully already. Your father wouldn't have allowed you to be introduced to Mr. Johnson if he wasn't eligible."

"Of course Frank's eligible, and wealthy too, but he's American. Mama wants me to marry into English nobility, but with all the available titled gentlemen marrying American heiresses, what can a girl do?"

Smiling her reply, Lucy gazed across the room. Her aunt signalled to them. "I think your mother wants us."

When Cecilly didn't react, Lucy followed the direction of her gaze. Quickly, she realised her cousin's attention was on a gentleman coming towards them. When he reached them he gave a curt bow.

"Good afternoon, ladies. Forgive my impertinence, but allow me to introduce myself. I am the Comte D'Every, at your service." He clicked his heels and nodded his head.

Lucy didn't know what to say. She understood a gentleman should not speak to ladies until a formal introduction had been made. Furthermore, they were under strict instruction from Lady Grant not to speak to anyone outside of their acquaintance. She noted his soft, accented voice and suspected he was of Belgian extraction. Pressing her lips together, she watched his steely grey eyes widen as he gazed admiringly at Cecilly over the hand she had offered him.

Swiftly, she glanced across the crowded room towards her aunt, who had her lorgnette to her eyes. As the older cousin and chaperone, Lucy knew she had to do or say something. She glanced back at Cecilly, who was fluttering her eyelashes and letting out girlish giggles in response to the compliments the comte was showering upon her. In desperation, she tugged Cecilly's arm. "Your mother wishes to speak to you immediately."

Again Cecilly ignored her.

"Excuse me," a strong male voice said. Lucy's heart skipped at the mellow, but not unfamiliar, sound. "I believe the ladies are needed elsewhere."

It seemed that Hardie had come to her rescue. She caught a gleam in his eyes and secretly hoped it was for her. *Was it his uniform or his clean chiselled jaw and lack of moustache?* She asked herself, then she recalled the navy only gave permission for a full-set. She tried to imagine him with a beard, but preferred the clean-shaven man standing before her.

The comte released Cecilly's hand and bowed. "I hope I may have the pleasure of meeting you again, Miss Grant."

Cecilly fluttered her lashes as he left, then switched her attention to the tall, naval officer. "I don't think I have the pleasure of your acquaintance, sir."

The smile which crossed his face brought warm creases around his eyes. His dimpled chin lifted. Lucy thought he looked even more handsome than at their first meeting. But was he now looking at Cecilly?

He glanced briefly back at Lucy. "Miss Mainwaring, perhaps you could be prevailed upon to make the introductions?"

Lucy's heart pounded as she uttered the required formalities, emphasising Cecilly's position as Sir Leyster Grant's daughter, and she hoped her reddening cheeks would go unnoticed.

"My pleasure, Miss Grant," he responded, "but regrettably our acquaintance for the moment must be short. Please understand, I'm only a messenger, but you *are* required to attend her ladyship."

Together the girls turned their heads and gazed across the crowded room. Lady Grant glared back at them. Excusing themselves, they edged their way towards her.

"He's very handsome, Lucy. Where have you been hiding him? I'm sure he likes you. I'm bursting to know how you met him," Cecilly whispered. "Confound Mother!"

* * * *

The girls retired to rest after the embassy reception. Lucy had been surprised by Cecily's urgency to go to their respective rooms, but welcomed the privacy. Alone at last, she sat in front of her mirror and gazed at her reflection. Her thoughts were of Hardie. She knew little of him, but the shortness of their acquaintance didn't seem to matter. When she closed her eyes, she saw his image and yearned to see him again.

She had no idea how long she sat languishing in her dreams. But her fairy tale was shattered by Cecily, who bounced into the room and threw several ball gowns onto the bed. "Try these on."

"They're yours. They won't fit."

"You haven't tried them on yet."

"There's no point. Besides, we've got to attend your mother at seven."

"At least try, Lucy, please. Do it for me. Promise you'll select two or three and try them on."

"I'm wearing the cream."

"Oh, no you're not! It's about time you had a little romance in your life, and if that means turning Lieutenant-Commander Hardie's head, then your old gown simply won't do."

Lucy stiffened. Her cousin's words had hit a weak spot.

"Please, Cousin, you've got to do this for me."

"For you?"

"Yes, Papa received a telegram today. Frank is coming to London. He could be here tomorrow or the day after." She clasped her hands together and squealed. "I'm so excited I could jump over the moon!"

"I'm very pleased for you. I've heard so much about Mr. Johnson that I'm very anxious to meet him. But why is it so important what I wear?"

"Can't you see?"

Lucy shook her head.

"Undoubtedly, Hardie will ask us both to dance, so you must look your best. Although I'd rather dance all night with Frank, I shall have to oblige Hardie. Papa would wish it. Frank will just have to accept that, but I can't have *your* navy officer hanging around *me* all night, can I? You must look so lovely that Hardie won't be able to take his eyes off you and if he stays with you, I can spend all my time with Frank. It's been so long since I've seen him. I'm sure he'll propose, and if Mama and Papa agree, by the end of tomorrow night's ball, Frank and I could be engaged!"

"And you really want to marry him?" Almost before she had finished her question, Lucy realised she didn't need to hear Cecilly's answer. The way her cousin's eyes lit up at the hint of the man's name left her in little doubt as to the depth of her affection.

Inwardly she admired her cousin's demonstration of love and wondered why she couldn't show her own feelings more openly. Perhaps it had been her restrictive upbringing and the sudden death of her mother. Her father never allowed himself to be close to her. He always shunned any affection she had given him and had never taken her into his arms to comfort her, even on the day of his wife's funeral.

Cecilly was so different: spontaneous, demonstrative, and outgoing, if somewhat inclined to selfishness. But Lucy found she could excuse Cecilly's self-centeredness as youthfulness. Convinced the responsibilities of marriage and motherhood would steady Cecilly, she shared her cousin's joy and returned her embrace.

"There is a problem. Frank hasn't...he's not formally proposed yet." She grabbed Lucy's wrists. "He's such a gentleman. He asked Papa's permission last summer, but my parents refused. There have been discussions, but Papa's been so stodgy over the whole matter. It's because Frank is American, and Mama doesn't like Americans. But if I could get him to offer for me, I know he'd never go back on his word, even if I have to wait until I'm twenty-one. I'd be engaged and the happiest girl in the world."

"Of course," Lucy said, slightly concerned that Frank might not be the best choice of husband for her cousin. But she decided to reserve her judgement until she had met the gentleman.

"Now you know why I've got to be alone with Frank."

"Is that wise?"

Cecilly gave out a long sigh. "Sometimes I think you've lived in the countryside too long. It's addled you brain. How can he propose in a room full of people?"

"I'm sure some men have managed it." Lucy chuckled.

"Perhaps, but if you could at least distract Hardie for a while, it might help. Please, Lucy, try on these gowns and surprise me."

"Very well, shall I call your maid?"

"No, Monique's busy—I'll help you. It's the least I can do if you're going to grab Hardie's attention. You know, he's very good-looking." She started to unfasten Lucy's gown, then peeking around her shoulder made an impish grin in the mirror. "I must find out more about your Lieutenant-Commander."

"My? What nonsense...we only met this morning. He knows nothing about me."

"No matter, he's interested. I *know* about these things. Men know what they like when they see it."

Lucy struggled into the first of the gowns, and Cecilly did up the back fastenings.

"You think I'm silly, don't you?" Cecilly said to Lucy's reflection in the mirror. "Oh, you needn't look away; I know I am sometimes. I can't help it, but I've learned to recognise one thing since I've been out." She stretched up on tip-toe and whispered, "Lust."

"How can you use such a word?"

"I can and I do!" A self-satisfied grin spread over Cecilly's face. "It's simple—men want women. Young women. Pretty women. And they want us even more if we're slightly...unobtainable. You know what I mean?"

Despite her five years seniority, Lucy wasn't entirely sure what her cousin was implying.

"Men love to flirt," Cecilly explained. "They enjoy winning us over. It's like a sport to them.

They shower us with gifts until we reluctantly surrender. I've seen it happen dozens of times over the past year. And watched some of the most unlikely men make utter fools of themselves in the process."

"The game of love and marriage can have some surprising turns and bring together some apparently oddly-matched couples. It is said, 'Marry in haste and repent at leisure.' For that reason alone, it's important to choose wisely before you rush into marriage. You are still very young."

"Yes, as everyone keeps reminding me, but I didn't expect to hear it from you. I thought you understood me. I was so glad when you decided to join us in London, and I'm dying for you to meet Frank. If only Mama and Papa had allowed Frank to propose to me last summer, I could be planning my wedding already, or perhaps I'd be married by now."

"Perhaps they considered it better for you to wait?"

"Wait! I'm sick of waiting!"

"But they only want the best for you—"

"Frank is the best for me. He's from one of the richest families in New York, so Papa can't object about money. However, he doesn't have a title, which annoys Mama, but American's don't have titles, do they? And he loves me."

"Do you love him?"

"Oh, Lucy, more than anything. If only we could be married, I'd be so happy."

"Then I hope it is all settled soon."

"Thank you, dear Lucy. *You* are the only person who understands how I feel. I just hope one day you'll find someone like my Frank."

"I think I would have to be extremely lucky."

"What about Hardie? I'm sure he likes you. I saw it in his eyes this afternoon."

"Really? Surely not!" Lucy's heart skipped a beat, but she didn't want to be drawn into a long conversation about her feelings for a man she hardly knew. "This blue velvet gown is very becoming. It fits my waist very snugly."

"At last," Cecilly declared gleefully, "I knew one of them would be right for you. Today I feel like your fairy godmother." She adopted a dramatic wand-waving pose. "Cinderella, you shall go to the ball and meet your Prince Charming." Her magic spell cast, she collapsed in a fit of laughter onto a low boudoir chair.

Lucy gazed at her full-length reflection in the mirror, and realised for the first time in her life, she looked beautiful.

Chapter Two

Lucy had just changed into a plain evening gown for dinner when both girls were summoned to attend her ladyship. They found her in the library, sitting upright in an armchair with a stern look on her face. As they crossed the room and came to stand in front of her, Lucy was convinced they were going to be rebuked over something but didn't know what.

"You wished to speak to us, Mama?"

"Girls, this afternoon I saw you make the acquaintance of the Comte D'Every." Her lips thinned as she spoke. "I understand he came in the company of the Belgian delegation and will be present at tomorrow night's ball. You must have nothing to do with him."

Lucy stole a meaningful glance at Cecily but didn't speak. Cecily's mouth dropped open, but she, too, remained silent.

Lady Grant rose from her armchair. "Cecily, I forbid you to dance with him. As you have already made his acquaintance, you must pay him the common courtesies should he address you directly. However, you will not behave as you did this afternoon."

Cecily turned a vivid shade of scarlet.

"Your father tells me Mr. Johnson will be in town tomorrow. We shall be pleased to see him.

Our enquiries about his family are complete, and I am pleased to say should he make you an offer, you have our permission to accept."

"Mama!" Cecilly ran into her mother's arms, all sign of her previous censure gone. "Do you think he'll actually propose?"

"Of course he will. The young man wouldn't cross the Atlantic unless he intended to pursue his suit. One only has to read his letters to know he adores you, and no wonder, for you are perfectly lovely." She paused and her expression sharpened. "You've not decided against him, have you?"

"Of course not, Mama, but what if he doesn't propose?"

"My dear girl, if you want to marry the man, you must see that he does."

Cecilly squealed her delight and kissed her mother's cheek. Several moments later, she asked, "What about Lucy?"

Lady Grant turned and began scrutinising her niece. "We must take you in hand. Your gown," she sighed, "is rather unbecoming. I'm afraid the rector's frugal allowance for a woman's apparel is completely inadequate. You cannot possibly manage on so limited a wardrobe in London. He kept your dear mother in a similar position. She never had a decent gown to her name, as far as I can recall."

Deeply embarrassed and hurt by her ladyship's remarks, Lucy moved to her father's defence. "Papa and I live in a country parish. What's suitable there may seem out of fashion here in London."

"Absolutely out of fashion," Lady Grant declared as she circled Lucy once more. "We must purchase a new wardrobe for you and make a few suitable introductions."

The thought of being placed under Lady Grant's wing and pushed in the direction of suitable introductions did not sit well with Lucy. But, as she reminded herself, she had agreed to be a companion to Cecilly and felt she had to oblige her ladyship.

"It is one's Christian duty to help one's less fortunate relatives, do you not agree, girls?"

Cecilly nodded. "Would it be acceptable to dance with Lieutenant-Commander Hardie tomorrow night?" Out of her mother's sight she winked at Lucy.

"I see no objection. He's your father's new aide and from a good family."

"Thank you, Mama. I met him at the reception this afternoon. I think he likes Lucy."

"That cannot be!" Lucy shook her head. "Cecilly is imagining things. I hardly know the gentleman."

"I hadn't considered Lord Devincourt's son." Lady Grant paused and tilted her head to one side. "He's eligible, but there's not much chance of the estate or the title. There's an older brother with offspring. Most likely Hardie wants an heiress, which might explain why he hasn't married yet. Although there are plenty of English girls from good families, most have little fortune. Titled gentlemen have chosen wealthy American brides in recent years, whilst our English debutantes seem to lose their hearts to Americans. By all means encourage him, Lucy. As a matter of fact, he would suit you very well. But, for your own sake, don't raise your hopes."

* * * *

London Society offered the wealthy an extravaganza of opulence. Frank Johnson had experienced his first taste of the whirlwind of social gatherings the previous year. Once it was known that he possessed wealth—and, therefore, eligibility—many society families had been anxious to introduce their nubile daughters to him. At Queen Charlotte's Ball he had met Cecilly Grant. By the time the royal yacht was tied up at Cowes Regatta, Frank had lost his heart to her. He had pleaded with Sir Leyster for permission to propose, but his request was refused. Cecilly had only just come out and Lady Grant was convinced there would be other offers.

When his father had required him to return to America, Frank had left London, but only after promising Cecilly he would return the following spring. Thus in bright sunshine, he strolled down Oxford Street, stopping briefly to browse in the new shop frontages as he made his way towards Marble Arch. He had been toying with an idea for several weeks. His family wished to meet Cecilly before a marriage took place, but Mr. Johnson Senior's health prevented him from making the sea-crossing.

Frank's plan was simple: to persuade the Grants to spend some time in New York, where he hoped a permanent understanding between the two families could be made. His feelings for Cecilly were unchanged, as he had explained in his many letters to her. Cecilly's letters had remained polite and brief. He was convinced Lady Grant had censored every word.

He hailed a motor-taxi. "Where to, sir?" the driver asked.

Frank was about to reply Grosvenor Place, but glancing at his pocket watch realised it was too early to call at the Grants' house, no matter how much he wanted to see Cecilly again. On a whim he said, "The White Star Offices."

"Oceanic House, sir, Cockspur Street?"

Frank nodded.

* * * *

Later that morning, the ladies received Frank in the drawing room. "When did you arrive in London, Mr. Johnson?" Lucy asked after the formalities of introductions were over.

"Yesterday," he drawled, "I berthed on the *Olympic* and took the boat train from Southampton late last night. She's a fine ship. Have you sailed on her, Miss Mainwaring?"

"Miss Mainwaring is up from the country, Mr. Johnson," Lady Grant explained. "She's had few opportunities to broaden her mind with overseas travel."

Lucy cringed inwardly at her aunt's patronising manner. She hoped her feelings didn't show in her face as she saw no shame in her work as a governess on the Continent. Time abroad had enabled her to improve her proficiency in French and German. But this wasn't the time to consider her feelings. She was more concerned about Cecilly. The girl had fallen remarkably silent since Mr. Johnson had been announced. But Lucy knew from her cousin's glowing expression that the object of Cecilly's affection stood before them.

Instead of taking part in the conversation, Cecilly fluttered her eyelashes every time Frank looked at her, which was often.

"You should visit America, Miss Mainwaring," he suggested. "New York society can be very stimulating."

"We've heard that 'over-exuberant' is a more fitting description," Lady Grant said. "Didn't Mrs. Astor report that some of the entertainment belonged under a circus tent rather than in a gentlewoman's house?"

Frank coughed and covered his fine, golden moustache with his hand. He took a few paces around the drawing room before answering. "True, a few years ago. More in my father's day, I'd say, but now we have a *new* Mrs. Astor. Madeleine's a delightful girl."

His remark cut the room. Lady Grant gave him a severe look of disapproval. He stiffened and swallowed hard.

Initially Lucy felt sorry for him, for she knew how easy it was to make a mistake when trying to create a good impression. But surely the censure poured on John Jacob Astor IV for divorcing his wife and marrying a girl younger than his own son was common knowledge on both sides of the Atlantic? Lucy had read that the outcry in New York society had been so great that the newlyweds were forced to travel abroad. Furthermore, a man of Mr. Johnson's standing should have known better, she reasoned, than to mention divorce in front of ladies.

As the silence grew more uncomfortable, she felt obliged to step in. "Mr. Johnson, you mentioned your recent Atlantic crossing on the *Olympic.* Have you any plans to sail on her new sister ship, the *Titanic*? She'll be making her maiden voyage soon."

Relief spread quickly across his face. "Indeed I have, Miss Mainwaring. Who would miss sailing on the world's largest and most luxurious liner? They say she's a floating palace. The most astounding achievement in naval architecture and marine engineering the world has ever seen. Why, her construction is so advanced, it's said she's practically unsinkable. I can't wait to sail on her."

"This new ship is operated by the White Star Line, Mr. Johnson. We always sail on Cunard vessels." Lady Grant said.

Again Lucy felt for the young American. It was almost as if he couldn't put a foot right when addressing her ladyship.

"How I would love to sail to America," Cecily exclaimed, clapping her hands together. "It would be so exciting!" She fluttered her eyelashes at

Frank yet again. Now it was Cecilly that Lucy despaired over, privately wondering if all women behaved like her cousin when they were in love.

Lady Grant stood up, which Lucy acknowledged should have been a signal for their caller to leave. But Mr. Johnson appeared to ignore the gesture. With a severe expression on her face, her ladyship crossed to the fireplace and rang the bell. When the butler entered, he had a visiting card on his silver salver and presented it to his mistress. Peering at the card, Lady Grant looked anxious. "You will have to excuse me for a few moments."

As soon as Lady Grant left and the butler closed the door, Cecilly leapt to her feet and threw herself at Frank. "Darling, you don't know how I've missed you."

"Cecilly...we're not alone," Frank gasped.

"Don't mind Lucy, she knows all about us." She stretched up on tip-toe and pecked him on the cheek.

Lucy flushed. She was expected to chaperone Cecilly in her ladyship's absence. She tried to look anywhere except at them and prayed Lady Grant didn't return and catch the pair cooing like turtle doves. Eager for any distraction, she was drawn to the visitor's card which Lady Grant had left on the table. Her eyes ran over the neat writing. *Lieutenant-Commander Hardie*. Her senses heightened in anticipation of another meeting.

The double doors swung open and the butler announced the lieutenant, who stepped into the room. Lucy's hand flew to her mouth. She half-expected Lady Grant to be following in the officer's wake, but the doors closed behind him. Cecilly and Frank sprang apart and looked in opposite directions from each other.

"Hardie," Cecilly gulped, "allow me to introduce Mr. Frank Johnson of New York."

"Delighted to make your acquaintance, sir." Hardie replied as he strode towards the American.

"And I yours," Frank said as they shook hands.

"When did you arrive in London, Mr. Johnson?" Hardie asked.

"I got in late last night."

"And the voyage? Calm seas, I trust?"

The way Frank smiled, Lucy thought he looked relieved there was no censure in Hardie's voice. If the officer had seen inappropriate behaviour from the young couple as he entered the room, at least he wasn't showing his disapproval publically, which pleased her.

However, there was no time for Frank to reply with more than a nod, as the butler opened the door and Lady Grant came in. "Hardie," she called across the room to him. "Are *these* the papers Sir Leyster referred to?"

Quickly Hardie took the large brown paper package from her. "I'm sure they are, Lady Grant, but if I could check them through before I leave?" She agreed, and he removed himself to the far side of the room, where he began sifting through the documents.

"Mr. Johnson, will you be attending the embassy ball this evening?" Lady Grant asked.

"Sure...I mean...of course," he muttered.

"Then we shall look forward to seeing you there."

It was obvious to Lucy that her ladyship's remark was intended as a parting one. Frank had stayed nearly half an hour, ten minutes longer than was considered polite for a morning call. But did he realise he was expected to leave? When he didn't move, Lady Grant said, "Will you excuse us, Mr. Johnson? The young ladies and I have an appointment in Bond Street."

But still Frank remained rooted to the spot.

"Goodbye, Mr. Johnson." She tugged the bell pull. When the butler entered, she announced, "Mr. Johnson is leaving."

After Frank's departure the conversation dwindled. Cecilly said nothing, her low spirits evident from her face. Lady Grant appeared vexed when she said, "That young man has a great deal to learn about conducting himself in society."

Hardie had repacked the parcel of documents and was about to leave when Lucy drew him to one side.

"Thank you for being so understanding when you arrived. I should have been a better chaperone." She had overcome her initial nervousness and was glad her usual self-confidence had been restored.

"I'm sure no harm was done, although Miss Grant appears to be missing the gentleman's company already."

Lucy nodded as she gazed into his eyes. Inwardly she felt a tingling sensation beginning in her stomach. Standing before her in his dark officer's uniform she couldn't help but admire him. She shook herself back to reality, relieved she could speak of Cecilly rather than herself. "She's been waiting for Mr. Johnson's visit for so long. I'm afraid patience isn't one of my cousin's virtues."

"Perhaps the prospect of the ball tonight will console her?" He raised a questioning eyebrow. "Personally I'm looking forward to it immensely."

Surprised by his last comment, Lucy felt her heart skip. Secretly she hoped his anticipated enjoyment included her. "Cecilly will be fine once she hears the dance music."

"Are those papers satisfactory?" Lady Grant asked as she approached them.

"Most certainly, Lady Grant." Hardie said as she came to stand beside him.

"And how is your dear father? I've not seen Devincourt in town for a long time."

Hardie looked at Lady Grant directly. "My father prefers his estate of late and does not enjoy travelling to town."

"And your brother, is he with him?"

"No, he remains in Kashmir and is likely to be resident there for some time to come."

"But your nephews—surely they are at school here in England?"

"I'm afraid not. Their education is of great concern to my father. He does not approve of private tutors. He would rather have them at Eton where all the Devincourts have been educated."

Lady Grant's frowned, nodding agreement. "I can understand his concern. So are all of your brother's family abroad?"

"Yes, my lady, my sister-in-law insisted on accompanying my brother and taking the boys with her."

"At least Devincourt has you, and for his sake, I hope your present posting keeps you in England. Please remember us to him on your next visit."

"I will carry your good wishes to him when I next visit."

Although she had taken no part in the conversation Lucy felt drawn to the man. She admired his friendly manner and the ease with which he had fielded Lady Grant's questions. Standing close to him she wanted to reach out and caress his strong jawline, even run her finger across his lips. *What am I thinking?* The sound of her name brought her out of her daydream. She gave Hardie a brief farewell and managed to smile. As the door closed behind him, her heart sank and her stomach tightened.

* * * *

As soon as Mr. Johnson left, Lucy realised the appointment in Bond Street was a fabrication. She assumed Lady Grant had made it up to get rid of him. Perhaps she didn't favour him as a prospective son-in-law, but that wasn't the picture she had painted to Cecilly when she had openly encouraged her to get him to propose. It all seemed very bewildering to Lucy. If Mr. Johnson did not meet Lady Grant's expectation as a suitable husband for her daughter, why was she allowing Cecilly to encourage him?

Lucy had plenty of time to mull over the problem as Lady Grant made the girls rest in preparation for the ball. The answer was probably her aunt's prejudice against new money. Lucy had no idea how wealthy her uncle really was.

Sir Leyster held a government appointment in the diplomatic service, yet whether he worked to provide for his family or simply because he wanted to serve his nation, she didn't know. She had never heard him speak about his appointment but knew he spent most of his days at an office in Whitehall.

The girls were lying on the bed in Cecilly's room in their undergarments, having removed their corsets. Lucy had a dressing gown around her shoulders, and Cecilly had a cashmere shawl around hers. Thinking Cecilly had drifted off to sleep, Lucy opened one of the magazines she had brought with her. However, Cecilly only had her eyelids closed. "Don't you think Frank is handsome?"

"He's a fine looking young man and most amiable." Lucy continued to flick over the pages of her magazine.

"And I'm going to marry him regardless of what Mama says about him!"

"Perhaps your mother was a little harsh this morning, when she began pointing out some of Frank's shortcomings, but—"

"He doesn't have any!"

"No one is perfect, Cecilly, we all have our faults. Frank's not used to English society, that's all. So, you must help him. Be his guide but never let him know it, and I'm sure you'll both be very happy."

"I'm so glad you're my friend. I'm so fortunate to have you and Frank." She grabbed Lucy's hand and squeezed it affectionately. "And don't you just love his American voice?"

Although she had a good ear for language, Lucy didn't favour the American east coast accent. However, she didn't want to upset Cecilly. "I understand the Americans have a range of dialects as diverse as those here in England, but I can't say that I like the way they seem to elongate their vowels."

"I think the way they speak is divine. I'd love to go to New York with Frank, after we're married, of course."

As Cecilly was silent for a few moments, Lucy thought that this time Cecilly really had fallen asleep. She glanced across at her and noticed her cousin's eyes were closed. But just as she was settling herself once more to read, Cecilly blinked several times.

"I'm not tired in the slightest. I'm bored." She pushed herself up onto her elbows. "Why don't you read something from your magazine? It might help pass the time."

"Do you really want me to?"

"Of course I do, silly goose. Is there anything about that new ship Frank mentioned? What did he call her?"

"The *Titanic*."

* * * *

Lucy took one last glance at herself in the cheval mirror. The deep midnight-blue velvet of her borrowed gown proved a perfect foil for her colouring. The straight, almost tubular skirt clung to her hips, whilst the deep pleating into the back panel made sitting easier than it appeared. The high waistband brought the velvet right up to her bust and made the Venetian point lace appear dainty as it fell from her shoulders. She stepped out onto the landing and waited for Cecilly.

Framed in the doorway, Cecilly appeared in a gown of gold brocade. The high-waist, tight-fitting bodice was trimmed with net and lace. Her train was longer than Lucy's but caught to the sides of her dress to emphasize the slimness of her hips. Her hem-line revealed a touch of lace, and she wore matching shoes.

"Didn't I promise we would look ravishing tonight?" She gave Lucy an impish grin.

Picking up her skirt, Lucy followed Cecilly downstairs. It was a moment she wanted to savour. Tonight she was moving in different circles. She felt a long way from the rectory and reality.

The embassy reception hall surpassed her expectation. Cecilly's coming-out ball had been grand, but the sumptuous decorations in the entrance hall of this event created a glorious spectacle.

"You must wear the train down," Cecilly insisted as they made their final preparations in the powder room. "The gown doesn't hang correctly otherwise." She beckoned the maid and asked her to attend to the buttons. Lucy smiled; left to her own devices she would not have bothered, but she was a guest and as a member of the Grant party it would be bad manners to appear awkward.

After they had been announced and presented to the ambassador, Sir Leyster left them. As the ladies entered the ballroom, Lucy gazed in wonder at the magnificence of her surroundings. Huge garlands of spring flowers embellished every corner, intermingled with swathes of pale lemon ribbons. Ladies in elaborate ball gowns with sparkling tiaras chatted in groups or walked elegantly by on the arm of a gentleman. So many men wore dress uniform that Lucy thought their gold braid almost relegated those in black evening attire to the ranks of the bland. She breathed in deeply, trying to savour the atmosphere of London Society, and wondered if she would ever experience anything as fine again.

Within a few minutes Frank appeared and claimed the dance Cecilly had promised him. As they took up position and waited for the music to strike up, Lucy watched them from the side of the ballroom. What a fine couple they made as they twirled gracefully around. His height, slender frame, and fair hair perfectly complemented her pretty femininity.

Remaining beside Lady Grant, Lucy felt out of place. Despite her aunt's introductions to a number of gentlemen, she received no invitations to dance. Being newly arrived in town and not known, or perhaps the fact that she had not come out as Cecilly had done, may have explained her social isolation. She dismissed both reasons and decided it was her poor relation status which kept most eligible gentlemen at bay.

She smiled and nodded throughout Lady Grant's intermittent conversation with other middle-aged matrons. Inevitably Cecilly was the main topic, as they watched her waltz in Frank's arms until the couple disappeared amongst the ever increasing numbers of dancers. There was nothing else to do except stand in silence. It was almost a relief when Lady Grant leaned towards her. "Where is Sir Leyster? Can you see him?"

Stretching on tip-toe, Lucy scanned the room, "I'm sorry, I can't see him."

But she did see the Comte D'Every approaching them and cringed. His evening dress was immaculate and his rank evident from his jewel. She tried to warn her aunt by tapping her arm, but the man was in front them of them before she could speak.

"Good evening, Lady Grant, Miss Mainwaring." He bowed his head. "May I have the honour of dancing with Miss Mainwaring?"

Lucy coloured, grateful he had addressed her ladyship instead of her.

Lady Grant lifted her head, almost sneering at the gentleman. "I'm afraid Miss Mainwaring is engaged for the entire evening."

His steel grey eyes turned cold as he looked directly at Lucy. "What a pity. The gentleman in question must be a fool to abandon such loveliness when the night is yet young."

Lucy's colour deepened. She hated lies and was moved to speak, but prudence kept her silent. She didn't want to dance with him. *If only Hardie would come and rescue me, as he's done before.*

The Comte D'Every's lips whitened. He turned swiftly and strode away.

"I will not tolerate that interloper." Lady Grant said as she squinted around the room. "Where is Sir Leyster? He must be in one of the card rooms. Follow me and stay close."

Dutifully Lucy followed as her ladyship strode into one of the smaller rooms where men stood in groups, deep in conversation. Lucy's eyes went straight to Hardie, and she took a deep breath. His dress uniform was perfectly sculptured to his broad shoulders, his hair glistening like a raven's wing. But as she was silently admiring him, he turned and caught her looking at him. Embarrassed, she blushed and tore her gaze away.

Sir Leyster excused himself from his company and approached the ladies. "Is there something wrong, my dear?"

Lady Grant drew him to one side and whispered behind her fan. Lucy knew it was wrong to eavesdrop, but she felt awkward and would rather have been back in the ballroom, had it not been for the encounter with the comte. Something was troubling her about him, triggered by his recent appearance. She thought hard for a few moments. He had known Cecilly's name at the embassy reception the previous afternoon, although they had not been introduced. And tonight, he had addressed her by name. *Why would a man of his rank be interested in me?*

She couldn't hear what her uncle and aunt were saying. However, she did see her uncle signal to his aide, who came over to them. Sir Leyster turned towards him and a brief conversation passed between them. She watched Hardie nodding his agreement to his superior. *Was he receiving orders?*

Lady Grant left the two men and rejoined Lucy. "I believe we have resolved the problem," she said.

Lucy wanted to ask what had been said, but she knew that would be impolite. Hardie broke away from Sir Leyster and stepped towards her. Her heart began to beat rapidly. What was he about to say to her? The fine hairs at the base of her neck began to rise.

"May I have the next dance?" His dark eyes gazed at her, and she felt she was the only woman in the room.

He looked so dashing in his immaculate dress uniform that any woman, whatever her age, would be happy to stand up with him. Graciously she accepted his arm and allowed him to escort her back to the ballroom. It was exactly what she had hoped for, but her pleasure was dulled. *Is he under direct orders from Uncle Leyster to partner me?*

They didn't speak, but as they passed groups of single ladies in their white dresses gathered on the edge of the ballroom, Lucy noticed several envious looks on their young faces. The orchestra struck the first few bars of a waltz. One firm hand supported her back and the other held her hand as they moved in unison to the music.

"Read any good newspaper stories recently, Miss Mainwaring?"

Momentarily her cheeks pinked. Then realising his teasing was deliberate, she smiled up at him. As they danced gracefully around the ballroom, the tension within her melted away.

He proved an excellent dancing partner, a tactful conversationalist, and had the most engaging smile which exposed a near perfect set of teeth. She wanted their dance to last all evening, but as the music progressed she sensed his attention drifting elsewhere. *Was he watching for something or someone?*

"Are you engaged for the next dance?" he asked as the final chords of the waltz music drifted away. Lucy had no need to consult her dance card; she knew there were no further entries. She shook her head, expecting to be returned to Lady Grant.

"Would you care to sit down?"

"That would be most welcome. It is becoming rather hot in here, don't you agree?"

He nodded his reply and escorted her from the dance floor. It pleased her when he found them seats near to the conservatory. The air was cooler there. Also, they were some distance from the circle Lady Grant had gathered around her.

"Thank you for allowing me to spend some time with you, Miss Mainwaring. I hope you don't think me presumptuous, but I would very much like to know you better."

Lucy straightened her back. "Sir Leyster ordered you to escort me, didn't he? So there's no need to flatter me unduly."

"He did, and I wasn't." He moved his head to look at her directly, and his dark blue gaze held hers. "A duty must always be carried out to one's best ability. If it also gives pleasure, then so much the better."

Lucy tore her gaze away. So, was she to be no more than a duty to him? Disappointment curled its way up her spine. She had hoped to be more, but that didn't seem feasible in her present circumstances. To London Society she was a guest of the Grants and always introduced as a relative, but she was no more than a companion and chaperone. When her presence was no longer required, Lady Grant would probably send her back to the rectory.

"Please, do not feel obliged to spend the evening escorting me. I'm sure I won't be troubled by the gentleman again."

"Do not underestimate the Comte D'Every. He is astute, elusive, and has a knack for turning up in the most unexpected places. Ironically, tonight I am grateful to him for enabling me to enjoy your delightful company."

"Please, there's no need to flatter me." Lucy glanced away, caught a glimpse of D'Every coming towards them, and gasped.

"What's the matter?"

"I believe the comte is coming this way."

As Hardie looked over his shoulder, D'Every acknowledged him with a curt nod. However, it was the comte's steely glare that Lucy felt keenly. Her mouth went dry, and a chill crept down her spine. *Surely he's not going to ask me to dance again?* She grabbed Hardie's hand. A twisted smile crossed the comte's face, and he hurried away. Discreetly, Lucy loosened her grip and removed her hand from Hardie's.

Aware of her body heat rising and concerned her complexion might be developing blotches, she flipped open her fan. The cool air she was able to waft over her face helped ease her discomfort, although for the first time that evening she regretted wearing the borrowed blue dress. To make the gown fit, her corset had been laced tightly, perhaps too tightly. She feared she might swoon at any second.

"It's very hot in here," Lucy said.

"Would you like some air?"

"That would be most agreeable."

Trusting him completely, she placed her hand on the arm he offered, and he led her out of the public rooms towards the conservatory. Inside, they strolled along an avenue of palms and exotic plants towards the exit to the garden. Walking with her hand neatly tucked into the crook of his arm, she relaxed and regained some of her self-confidence. "Please forgive me for acting so rashly. I didn't think. He startled me."

"I understand. Perhaps we should talk of more mundane matters?"

Lucy smiled and breathed a sigh of relief. How wonderful it felt to be beside such a reassuring officer. "How long have you been attached to Sir Leyster?"

"Only a month. Previous to my present posting I was engaged in sea trials, and before that, I was at sea for several years."

"And which do you prefer?"

"I'm a sailor, and a sailor must go to sea."

Lucy smiled. "Although I was brought up in the countryside, I like the sea very much. Papa took me on several trips to the coast. I found the air very bracing."

"Many people do, Miss Mainwaring, but the sea can be very cruel."

"I assume you have braved many violent storms at sea, but have you ever been shipwrecked?" She knew it was an odd question, but she was curious to know more of his seafaring career.

"No, I am pleased to say I have always returned to harbour safe and sound. Shall we sit here?" He pointed to an iron bench beneath a window looking into the house. It was a secluded corner, the sort of place she expected to find Cecily and Frank.

For a brief moment she stopped to consider if she really ought to be alone in the conservatory with Hardie. But she was enjoying his company so much; she didn't want to ask him to return her to the ballroom and her aunt.

She sat down, looked up at him, and expected him to sit beside her. Instead he moved behind the bench. She craned her neck around to see what he was doing. From her seated position she couldn't see anything except his large frame hunched over. He appeared to be peering through the window.

"What are you doing?"

He made no reply.

The sound of footsteps approaching caught her attention, and she whipped her head around to see who was coming. Before she could make out who it was, a large hand covered her mouth and prevented her from crying out.

"Don't make a sound." Hardie's breath felt hot on her neck as he sat down.

Fear filled her. Had she misjudged his character? She didn't know what to do. *What is he doing to me?* The footsteps halted close by, only a few potted palm plants preventing them from being discovered. The strong smell of a burning cheroot pervaded the air as the intruder waited silently. Hardie's hand remained over her mouth as another set of footsteps clicked over the black and white tiled floor towards them. The person halted, and from behind the palms, two men spoke in French.

Lucy recognised one accent as very coarse, almost hard in tone. The other was more refined and slightly familiar. But the men spoke only briefly, until the common-voiced man was told to leave by his better educated partner. As his footsteps retreated, relief surged through Lucy's sensitive body, and her breathing steadied. It was only then that she became aware of the measured thud of Hardie's heartbeat as he pressed her against his chest.

With her lips crushed against the palm of his hand she had to take short, shallow intakes of air through her nose. His other arm clenched around her waist, pressing against her flesh through her gown, corset, and undergarments. She had no idea how long they remained on the bench, her hands grasping his arms, attempting to prise herself out of his grip. But, vicelike, he held onto her. Eventually, convinced he wasn't going to let her go, she relaxed, hoping he might lessen his hold on her if she put up no resistance.

"One man's gone," he whispered. "The other is still there. I don't think we've been spotted."

Lucy nodded, but she must have moved as a clink echoed through the conservatory. She looked down. The weighted train of her gown had slipped onto the tiled floor. Hardie removed his hand from her mouth, pulled her towards him, and kissed her.

Her body stiffened. Then she freed one hand and pounded him with her clenched fist. Ignoring her struggles, he continued to press his kiss upon her. Realising the futility of struggling, she let her body go limp again. *Was this what Cecilly meant about lust?*

She closed her eyes, not knowing what she wanted until, still embracing her, he lifted his mouth from hers. "He's gone. I'm so very sorry...it was all I could think of."

Her mouth dropped open as she felt his warm breath on her cheek. But in the dim light she couldn't see into his eyes. She felt confused and vulnerable.

"Can you speak French?"

Swallowing hard, she nodded.

"Did you follow their conversation?"

In the half-light, she could only make out the dark shadows of his face. "Yes," she breathed, trying to make sense of what had happened as she felt his grip on her tighten at her response. What had she done? Had she encouraged him in any way? Her head spun with the strange conversation she had overheard. What did it mean? She knew she shouldn't be here, not alone with him.

"Take me back...please."

Finally, he relaxed his hold and gently covered her hand with his. "Come," he urged, as he led her towards the door. But before they reached the exit, he stepped in front of her and pulled her into his arms.

"I'm sorry, Lucy, truly I am." He cupped her face in his hands and dropped a tender kiss on her lips. "We're probably being watched."

Chapter Three

After a brief word with his superior, Hardie whisked Lucy into a motor-taxi. "Don't look so worried. I won't take advantage of you."

"Why have we left the ball so early? I should have spoken to my aunt. She will be annoyed with me." But her protests were ignored as he ordered the driver to take the long route around Hyde Park.

"We must talk," he insisted as the vehicle pulled away. "I need answers to a few questions."

"You need answers! Don't I deserve an explanation for your behaviour in the conservatory and why we had to leave the ball so early?"

"Of course, and I promise I'll tell you all I can. But first, Sir Leyster says you speak French fluently. What exactly did those men say?"

She hesitated before replying. She wanted to trust him but how could she after the way he had behaved? And why had Sir Leyster agreed to them leaving together? Surely that too was most improper? However, since her uncle had sanctioned the arrangement, she decided to tell him all she had heard.

"I did follow what they were saying, but I don't know what it all meant. The first man was annoyed he'd been kept waiting. His French was refined, almost aristocratic, but with a slight accent. He asked the second man if he had the documents, but the German wanted his money before he parted with them."

"German! Why do you think the second man was a German? They both spoke French."

"He sounded a rough, common sort of fellow with poor French. His accent was strong. I couldn't place it, until I remembered hearing someone like him before. I'm convinced he was from Munich."

"Are you certain?"

She looked at him closely, his dark hair, his chiselled jaw, and his strong full mouth. He was a strikingly good-looking man, even in the dim light of the motor-taxi. But could she trust him? Lucy stared, hesitated, and doubted. Less than an hour ago he had kissed her as no other man had done before.

"Yes," she breathed and desperate to conceal the effect he had upon her, she turned her head towards the window. Outside they were rounding Marble Arch.

"Lucy, please look at me."

Unable to resist his tender plea, she turned back slowly, uncertain of her own feelings. She swallowed deeply, attempting to control the sensation surging through her body as if her nerve endings were on fire.

"Those men are spies. They sell information to the highest bidder. Thefts of highly confidential documents have taken place in London recently."

He had called her Lucy, and she liked the sound of it.

"Because of my ineptitude, you have witnessed a possible exchange of state secrets. Forgive me. I had no idea it would happen, but I must take full responsibility for my lack of foresight. I had no right to expose you to danger."

"Danger? What danger?"

"If those thieves believe you witnessed their involvement in spying activities, they may do you harm."

"Thieves! Can't the police arrest them?"

"The authorities need evidence and witnesses to bring charges."

"The German complained he had no safe place to stay. The other man, the well-spoken one, gave him an address: Twenty-three Saint John's Wood Road. Can't the police arrest him there?"

"I will pass the address on to the authorities, and he will be apprehended. He's probably only a courier. He'll be well-paid to keep silent whilst the real culprits remain at liberty."

"Tell me, is my uncle involved in catching spies?"

Hardie shifted in his seat. "I'm duty bound not to answer."

"But...I'm confused. Why were we in the conservatory? What were you looking for through the window?"

"You're very observant, Miss Mainwaring." He paused just long enough for Lucy to note he had returned to formalities between them. "As you appeared flushed, I thought a stroll might refresh you. When we were about to sit down, I saw a flash of light through the window. I knew that part of the embassy was closed to guests. I saw a man in the room, helping himself to the contents of the wall safe."

"You witnessed a theft?"

"Possibly, but I couldn't leave you alone. There wasn't time to escort you back to Lady Grant. Foolishly I thought I could observe the thief without involving you. The rest you know."

"I see," she murmured, disappointed by his explanation. "So you think you saw the second man, the German, taking the papers? And we heard him delivering them to—oh my goodness!"

"What's the matter? Are you unwell?"

"No, but I've just realised that man...the one smoking the cheroot. I'm sure it was the comte."

"That thought crossed my mind too, but I didn't get a good look at him. But none of this should have happened to you. Please accept my most sincere apologies, I acted impulsively and—"

"We cannot change what has happened." Lucy interrupted. Outwardly she had recovered her demeanour, but inwardly her thoughts were in turmoil. So much had happened in such a short time. As the motor-taxi stopped outside the Grant's town house, Lucy waited for Hardie to help her out of the vehicle and escort her to the front door.

"You must not discuss or tell anyone what we witnessed at the embassy tonight," Hardie's tone was serious. "Do I have your word that you will remain silent?"

"Of course."

* * * *

As they sat opposite each other in the library, Hardie assessed the situation. He wasn't prepared to leave Lucy alone, even at the Grants' house, until Sir Leyster returned and he could explain to him what had happened more fully.

Despite the misunderstanding and his somewhat improper behaviour, he had to acknowledge he liked Miss Lucy Mainwaring. He could not deny the warmth he had found when he held her close nor the pleasure his lips had enjoyed when they descended on hers.

He deeply regretted involving her, an innocent party, in an incident he should have avoided. And as he gazed silently at her, he became acutely aware of her vulnerability. Behind the veil of composure she had drawn since returning to the house, he wondered about her true feelings. Could he dare to hope that she might one day overlook his ill-judgement? Although guilt-ridden about involving her, he had no regrets about kissing her and dearly wanted to kiss her again. The more he knew of Miss Lucy Mainwaring, the more he wanted to know her better.

The silence was broken by movement outside in the hall. He watched Lucy jump slightly, then place one hand over the other as if to steady herself. The door flew open.

"Lucy!" Cecilly cried in an excited voice. "I must tell you, I can't wait a moment longer. Frank has proposed! I'm so happy. I don't think I shall be able to sleep a wink tonight."

As Lucy stood up, Cecily ran towards her, threw her arms around her cousin, and hugged her.

"We're not alone," Lucy said.

Cecily turned around and her mouth dropped open.

"Forgive the intrusion, Miss Grant, but I must speak to your father." He gave a curt nod to Lucy and strode out of the room, leaving the two cousins to talk.

* * * *

"My dear Lucy, I hope you weren't too put out leaving so early last night." Lady Grant buttered a slice of toast.

"Of course she wasn't, Mama." Cecily beamed. "Lucy was escorted home by Lieutenant-Commander Hardie."

Lucy hadn't said anything to anyone about the conservatory as she had promised Hardie to remain silent. But the more she dwelt on last night, the more she realised she should never have allowed him to take her there. What had happened was her own fault, and although she couldn't change what had passed between them, she didn't want to discuss the liaison with her aunt or cousin. The stolen documents were taken from an embassy; therefore, they must have had some significance to the government involved. However, she doubted if she would ever hear any more of the matter. But what of the kisses they had shared?

"Cecilly and I will be visiting this morning," Lady Grant announced.

"We're both anxious to spread the news about my engagement. You'll come too, won't you, Lucy? There are so many calls to—"

"That won't be possible," Lady Grant cut in. "Your father has asked to see Lucy in his study at noon."

"What about, Mama?"

"Cecilly, you must learn it is not ladylike to pry into business. That is for the gentlemen." She looked at Lucy. "I suppose it's something to do with your father."

Lucy's hand flew to her mouth. "Oh dear, has there been bad news from the rectory?"

"Goodness no, my dear. Sir Leyster simply wants to discuss your future, now that Cecilly is engaged."

* * * *

With time on her hands, Lucy decided to attend morning service.

"Excuse me, Miss Mainwaring, won't you be taking one of the footmen or maids with you?" the butler asked as she crossed the hall to leave.

"That won't be necessary," she assured him. "I'm quite used to attending church by myself. I shall only be across the square."

Although there were only a handful of people at the service, it didn't bother Lucy. Grateful for the solitude, she had time to think matters over. But once in church, her father's parting words came back to her as clearly as if he'd been preaching the sermon. "Do not allow your head to be turned by frivolous and extravagant ways."

Of course last night she had dreamt of Hardie. However, she had no illusions that his amorous attentions in the conservatory would be repeated today or any other day. His actions had been to fool thieves, taken on the spur of the moment, and without true affection.

She forced herself to be practical. She had no money, no dowry. Would that be important to a man of his standing? Quickly she forced herself to remember she was a vicar's daughter and a governess, not an heiress. And her future? Lady Grant had hinted that as a companion she was expected to remain in London until Cecilly's wedding, but afterwards? Return to the rectory or seek another teaching post?

As she walked back to the house, her thoughts were solely of Hardie. Could she hope? It was pleasant to do so, for already she was in great danger of liking him in a very special way. Despite the circumstances, she couldn't stop herself reliving his passionate kiss. She had enjoyed the strength of his arms around her and the warmth of his breath at the nape of her neck.

Lost in her thoughts, she was oblivious to the sounds of the street, until everything seemed to happen as once. A man cried, "Get out of the way!"

Strong hands grabbed her from behind and pulled her to the ground as a horse-drawn cab missed her by inches. Disorientated by the fall, she could barely make out the sound of clattering hooves and wheels retreating. The old cab did not stop. Several voices were calling to her, but only one was familiar and reassuring.

"Lucy," he repeated several times, then, "Miss Mainwaring, are you hurt?"

Everything was swimming. "Hardie, is that you?"

She felt strong arms sweep her off her feet and assumed they must be his. He must have carried her over the Grants' threshold, because she heard the butler say, "I asked Miss Mainwaring to take one of the footmen with her. I'll call a maid."

Once inside familiar surroundings, Lucy recovered quickly. Although the security of his arms around her was very comforting, she was grateful to feel the floor beneath her feet. "Thank you, Lieutenant-Commander, for your help."

"What were you doing out alone?" he demanded in an exasperated tone.

She found his censure hurtful. "Returning from church; am I supposed to have foreseen a horse bolting?"

"The driver whipped up his horse and headed straight for you. What happened to you was no accident. Didn't you hear it coming?"

"Not until it was almost upon me...I had other matters on my mind. Now perhaps you will excuse me?"

* * * *

Sir Leyster rose when Lucy entered his study. "Please, sit down. No need to stand on ceremony."

He placed a chair near to his desk as he spoke. "Have you recovered from your accident?"

"Yes...thank you," she managed to utter. Her stomach muscles clenched when she saw Hardie standing in front of the window. His face was creased with concern and he had his hands behind his back. Sir Leyster, too, looked tense as he hovered at her elbow until she sat down.

"Under no circumstances must you leave this house unaccompanied." Sir Leyster said.

Lucy swallowed deeply at her uncle's stern instruction. Seeing Hardie in the study had already unnerved her. Now, Sir Leyster's direct order added to her discomfort.

"Circumstances are different in town," he continued, "you must understand."

"Of course," she nodded, trying to appear more confident than she actually felt.

He resumed his seat behind his large mahogany desk and leaned towards her. "Were you hurt, my dear?"

She managed a brave smile, relieved his voice had softened. "Just mud and a few bruises."

"Perhaps, but you mustn't put yourself at risk. I promised your father I would look after you. And I still haven't heard your account of last night." He paused for a few moments. "I don't want to upset you, but could you tell me now?"

"Uncle Leyster," she looked pleadingly into his eyes, "I appreciate your concern but hasn't Hardie explained?" She glanced hopefully across at his tall figure, half-expecting him to leap once again to her defence.

"Yes, but I'd like you to tell me in your own words what you heard and saw in the conservatory. I'm not questioning why or what you were doing there, nor will I interrupt to ask questions. I just want to hear your account."

Lucy took a deep breath and began her story from where they entered the conservatory, describing all she had heard, but leaving out the part where Hardie kissed her.

Whilst she spoke, Sir Leyster sat back in his large leather chair. When she had finished, he turned to Hardie. "Was the thief apprehended?"

"Yes, he's a known criminal. As we suspected, he was hired for the job."

Sir Leyster's attention returned to Lucy. "My dear, you are family, and I am responsible for your welfare. I don't wish to alarm you, but Hardie is convinced that this morning's incident was no accident. Your person could be harmed. Often thieves are desperate men who will stop at nothing. You must not go out alone."

"But..." she looked at Hardie, silently asking for his support, "if we witnessed stolen documents being passed on, won't the thieves assume the information has been reported to the police?"

"If only it were that simple," Sir Leyster paused, as if to choose his words carefully. "A theft may have taken place last night, but it has not been reported. His Majesty's Government has no jurisdiction within an embassy. We cannot pursue the matter officially. However, these thieves pay no heed to international boundaries or laws. Courts of law require witnesses to give evidence in person. By threatening you, perhaps the thieves believe they can secure Hardie's silence."

A cold shiver crept the length of Lucy's spine as she realised the full implications of what he was saying.

"We are making travel arrangements," Sir Leyster continued. "In the circumstances it would be extremely prudent for you to accompany us. Finally, nothing of this conversation must be repeated to anyone. Do I have your full cooperation?"

"Of course."

He stood up and nodded across at Hardie, as if giving him leave to speak.

Hardie approached Lucy. "Could I have a few words with you, Miss Mainwaring?"

Anxiously she looked back at Sir Leyster.

"Stay, my dear," he urged. "Hear the man out."

The thud of the door closing behind Sir Leyster heralded a few uneasy moments for Lucy. She began to speak at the very same time Hardie did.

"Please, after you," he offered.

"I wanted to apologise; perhaps I misjudged your action this morning." She took in a deep gulp of air, then her words poured out. "I find it most distressing that anybody would deliberately cause me harm. I was rude to you this morning, I'm sorry, I—"

"Don't!" He paced the carpet. "It was my fault. You wouldn't have been involved at all if it hadn't been for my ineptitude!"

"Perhaps you exaggerate the danger?"

"I do not," he insisted. "I'm to blame. It is my duty to offer you my personal protection at all times."

"But that's impossible. How can you do that?"

"Marry me, Lucy, without delay."

Shocked and bewildered, she held her breath and stared back at him for several moments, until an overwhelming feeling of uncertainty swept over her like a gigantic wave. It felt wrong. She was not filled with the ecstatic joy she had anticipated feeling upon receiving her first offer of marriage. This wasn't the proposal she had imagined, it was barely a marriage proposal at all. She searched for inner strength, not daring to look at him, determined to keep calm and not give in to foolish fancy. Above all, reason must prevail, she tried to convince herself.

She rose from her chair. "We are hardly acquainted," she reminded him as she turned to face him. "You cannot profess to love me as a man should love his wife. I have no fortune to bring to our union. So, I must ask, is your proposal based solely on your sense of duty?"

He came a few steps closer and looked into her eyes. "If anything happened to you, Lucy, I would never forgive myself."

She ripped her gaze from his. "Do you want to marry me to satisfy your own conscience?"

He didn't answer.

"Don't patronise me, Hardie. I may only be the daughter of a country parson, but I do have my self-respect."

"I never doubted it."

She didn't know where her strength came from but knew she had to speak the truth. She fixed her eyes on his. "I have emotions and feelings, but my good sense tells me not to be influenced by a few kisses occurring in circumstances neither of us should have allowed to pass. To marry out of obligation is not a good starting point for marriage. Think of the future. Circumstances such as ours could so easily be construed into a situation where I would be blamed for entrapping you. I respect your sense of duty, and for the present, your loyalty is unquestionable, but I must be rational. My answer must be no."

Not waiting for his reaction she made for the door, her legs barely able to support her. *Why am I turning him down? If only I can reach the door. A marriage based on duty would be empty. If he makes a move towards me, takes me in his arms and kisses me as he did last night...I shall be lost to all reason.*

She didn't hear Hardie move. He wasn't coming after her. As she closed the door behind her, a sharp pain stabbed her chest. She had known him only three days, but it was long enough. From today, he would always hold a special place in her heart.

Chapter Four

Lucy stayed in her bedroom for most of the afternoon. She needed time to herself to think. How could her life have become so complicated in the space of a few days? Entering the conservatory with Hardie had been a bad decision, yet she could still feel the touch of his kiss on her lips when she closed her eyes. However, becoming embroiled in espionage by witnessing the theft of state secrets had been Hardie's doing. And the hansom cab incident? She couldn't blame him for that, but the thought that someone meant to threaten her—or worse, cause her serious harm—filled her with fear. But all these anxieties were nothing when she compared them to Hardie's proposal. If only he had said something about his feelings for her.

Occasionally she peered out of the window onto the Mayfair square beneath. Life was passing by outside on the street, with delivery boys riding bicycles and nurse maids wheeling their charges, but inside behind closed doors, Lucy's life was in turmoil. *I had to turn him down. I was right,* she kept telling herself. But in her heart, she knew she was deceiving herself.

The sound of a vehicle outside brought Lucy to the window again. The Grants' Rolls Royce halted below. The chauffeur held the rear door open as Cecilly and Lady Grant stepped onto the pavement.

Lucy took a step back from the open window. She didn't want her aunt or cousin to see her spying on them.

Half-expecting Cecilly to bounce into her room, Lucy braced herself. Somehow she had to mask her feelings and keep them hidden. She had turned the day's events over in her mind again and again without resolution, but knew she couldn't confide in her cousin. Whatever her feelings were for Hardie, Cecilly would not understand. Her cousin acted on impulse. She would hear the words, "Hardie has proposed," and jump to the conclusion that they were engaged. How could she explain she was not? That she had turned him down and in doing so had made herself utterly miserable.

She took a deep breath when she thought she heard Cecilly outside on the landing, but it was only the maid with a message that Lady Grant was about to serve afternoon tea in the drawing room and wanted her to join them. Lucy took a quick glance in the mirror. There were several red blotches on her face and she looked tired. Hopefully, Cecilly and her mother wouldn't notice.

Several minutes later, when Lucy entered the drawing room, Lady Grant smiled at her and indicated for her to sit down on a seat close to her own.

"We have had the most wonderful time," Cecilly said. "It's been so exciting telling everyone about my engagement."

Lady Grant poured the tea and handed a cup to each of the girls. Lucy had only taken a few sips of hers when her aunt launched into a long description of the morning visits, which included precise details about the splendid luncheon they had enjoyed at the duchess's house in Regent's Park.

"Oh, you should have been there, Lucy," Cecily sighed, "everyone wanted to know about Mr. Johnson and the wedding arrangements. Of course, I had to tell them that nothing was settled regarding the date or the venue, but everyone was so helpful with advice."

Lucy listened, nodded at the appropriate points, and realised neither her aunt nor Cecily knew about the hansom carriage incident or Hardie's proposal. Inwardly she breathed a sigh of relief and endured the conversation dominated by Cecily's wedding arrangements. Eventually, the Grant ladies settled on the best dressmaker and were discussing the merits of silk over satin when Sir Leyster joined them.

Having no part in the conversation, Lucy quietly observed her uncle. He took a few strides across the room and positioned himself with his back to the fireplace. He appeared to listen to the conversation between his wife and his daughter for several moments before he spoke. "My dears, your arrangements will have to be postponed for a while. There's to be a change of plan. We're all going to New York."

Lady Grant's forehead creased as she glared at her husband. "When? I haven't been consulted. When was this decided?"

"I took young Johnson to my club this afternoon." Sir Leyster paused and grinned with obvious pleasure at Cecilly. "The more I get to know the fellow, the more I like him."

Cecilly clapped her hands. "I knew you would, Papa. Oh, New York, I've always wanted to go there. It's so exciting!"

Lucy wondered whether her uncle's plans included her. He had said, "We're *all* going," but did her mean her too? New York, the gateway to America, held many attractions including entertainment, culture and commerce. The prospect of visiting the city sent tingles down her spine. She looked at her uncle and checked her excitement. She might be sent back to her father?

"Johnson's been planning a surprise for us. Of course, the fellow had to assume Cecilly wouldn't turn him down." Sir Leyster shot a meaningful glance in Lucy's direction as he spoke. Inside she winced at his reference to her declining Hardie's offer. She hoped her reaction to his pointed comment went unnoticed by the others.

"A surprise, Papa? You know how I love surprises." Cecilly leapt to her feet, clung to her father's arm, and bobbed up and down like an excited child.

"Johnson's keen to make the maiden crossing on the new White Star liner, so he's taken an option on a few staterooms. I considered the matter over luncheon and decided a trip to America wouldn't be out of the way. Did I mention, Maud, that I have been invited to speak at an international peace conference in New York?"

"No, I don't recall," Lady Grant replied, seated straight-backed, hardly moving a muscle.

Lucy glanced at her aunt's face, deep indignation appeared to be etched upon it. Feeling very much an outsider to the Grant's plans, Lucy kept her own counsel.

"Fits my plans tremendously," Sir Leyster added. "I've accepted the invitation to speak at Carnegie Hall on the twenty-first. So, Maud, get these girls packed. We're leaving on the boat train on the tenth."

"In one week!" Lady Grant gasped. "We can't possibly be ready to visit America in seven days."

"Nonsense," he said. "If the Admiralty can move half the fleet in less time, then you can move these girls."

"Lucy too, Papa? She is coming with us, isn't she?" Cecilly tugged her father's arm again.

He smiled affectionately down at her and patted her hand. "Rest assured, I have no intention of leaving Lucy behind."

* * * *

The following morning the official announcement of Cecilly's engagement appeared in the newspapers. Several congratulatory notes arrived with the first post.

"I'll leave you to deal with the replies, Maud," said Sir Leyster as they sat at the breakfast table with Cecilly and Lucy.

"Certainly. I'm sure the girls can help too. Lucy has a particularly neat hand."

As Cecilly's wedding took over the rest of the conversation between mother and daughter, Lucy remained silent and sipped her tea. Sir Leyster opened up a newspaper, buried himself behind it, and ignored any further questions. Several minutes later, he flopped the newspaper down on the table. "Lucy," he said, "I have received a letter from your father. There are a few matters I wish to discuss with you before I reply. Will you join me in my study when you have finished?"

"Of course, Uncle Leyster."

"Good, when you are ready." He smiled, rose, and quit the breakfast room.

"Oh, my dear Lucy, I do hope your father isn't demanding your return. We have so much to do. Your talent for organising and attention to detail will be invaluable over the next few days," Lady Grant said.

Lucy nodded. "I will help in whatever way I can."

"Then you had better attend Sir Leyster now. Immediately after he has finished with you, come back and help us. Goodness knows how we shall be ready in time to sail on that ship."

* * * *

Sir Leyster offered Lucy a chair. "I have received a letter from your father, but it's not him I want to talk about. This business with Hardie, it's causing me a degree of unease. He said you turned him down. He tried to explain to me why you refused him, but he wasn't very clear. Suffering from wounded pride, I believe. But seriously, I think you should reconsider."

Determined to choose her words carefully, Lucy thought for a few moments. "I know his offer is a generous one. I may not receive the like again, but...it's based on guilt. He feels responsible for me because of the embassy incident. Such a marriage would be no more than an arranged one."

Sir Leyster gripped the edge of his desk as he eased himself into his seat. "Some arranged marriages are very successful."

"And many are not."

"Marrying for love doesn't always fare any better."

"Perhaps not, but *I* expect to love the man I marry."

"And Hardie doesn't appeal to you?"

Lucy felt her cheeks go hot. "We're hardly acquainted."

"Not according to half of London. The half that listens to gossip, of course."

Lucy hand flew to her mouth. "Whatever do you mean?"

Sir Leyster leaned forward onto his elbows and clasped his hands together. "Rumours are rife. Hardie is being accused of compromising a young lady at the embassy ball, right under the nose of the family who was supposed to protect her. As yet, neither she nor the family have been named. Too much is being said to be idle gossip. I think someone is deliberately trying to undermine reputations."

"But who?" Before he could reply, Lucy realised she was being naive. "Comte D'Every?"

"Yes, my dear. I fear he is playing some sort of cat and mouse game with you both. He thought he saw Hardie compromising a young lady of good standing and is seeking to discredit him in society. As yet, your name has not been mentioned, but we must expect it will only be a matter of time before it is, and then your reputation will be at stake." He leaned forward across the desk. "I can't emphasize how fragile a young woman's reputation can be. It only takes one slur, even if she is totally innocent, and her future could be ruined. Respectability is hard to restore as one becomes a social outcast. I'm trying to make this absolutely clear to you because now that you have refused Hardie, other men may not be forthcoming."

Shocked by the possible repercussions her behaviour in the conservatory might have on the rest of her life, Lucy held her breath for a few moments. Letting it out with a long sigh she asked, "What am I to do?"

Sir Leyster raised his bushy eyebrows. "Reconsider, my dear. Hardie is a decent, upstanding, and reliable fellow. I have told him that as a member of my family I will provide you with a dowry."

"That's very generous of you, uncle. But aren't second sons supposed to look for heiresses?"

He leaned back in his chair and broke eye contact with her. After a few moments he said, "I wouldn't pay too much heed to that notion. Men who marry for money often get their just desserts."

His words, said as if he was thinking aloud, cut her keenly. Was he referring to someone close to her? "Forgive my impertinence, but were you thinking of my father?"

He looked surprised by her question. A muscle flickered around his mouth. "Your father and I do not see eye to eye on many matters. I thought my father acted harshly when he cut Mary off. I was up at Oxford at the time and powerless to help her. Your grandfather did not approve of the marriage, but they were determined to marry."

"Were they happy? Truly happy?"

Sir Leyster shrugged his shoulders. "I suppose so. Aren't most love matches in the beginning? But the future doesn't always live up to expectation. Mary yearned for children, but she wasn't blessed for many years. And there were long periods of separation when John went on missions to Africa and the Far East. Mary wanted to go with him, but he would never allow it. She was delighted when you were born. I think John was too. He never went abroad again, so possibly your arrival marked a turning point in their marriage."

No one had ever spoken to her about her parents' early married life. Her mother was the capable wife, who ministered to the sick and needy of the parish. As a small child she had endured her father's long sermons in silence in cold churches. Her parents had always been old to her. It was hard to imagine them as a young couple in love. "Thank you for being so honest."

"Do not dwell on a past, which is none of your doing. It's your future, Lucy, which should concern you. Hardie's a good fellow; honest, reliable and trustworthy. He'll stand by you. He'll treat you well and be a good father to your children. He's a man to be proud of."

She shifted nervously on her seat. Her misgivings about refusing Hardie had plagued her from the moment she had turned him down. His proposal had surprised her. But after she had refused him, she had wondered if she had done the right thing, as she found him very attractive. But how did he feel about her?

"He doesn't love me," she blurted out.

"Ah!" Sir Leyster clapped his hands together. "We have the problem in a nutshell. Hardie's a man after my own heart. I shouldn't think he's very good at expressing his feelings, especially towards women. But that doesn't mean he's insensitive. We men can be strange creatures. We even deceive ourselves sometimes. Only when we have lost, or think we've lost, someone do we discover our true feelings. And then it can be too late."

Lucy denoted a tinge of sadness, possibly regret, in his voice. She looked up into his eyes and realised they were a perfect match in colour to her own. "What do you suggest I do?"

He clenched the arms of his chair. "Tell Hardie you'll reconsider his offer. You know he's sailing with us to New York?"

Lucy felt her uncle's eyes scan her face quizzically. She gave a curt nod.

"It'll give you both a chance to get to know each other." He raised his bushy eyebrows. "You know, more than one marriage has been fixed during a sea-crossing. Give the man a chance, eh?"

Chapter Five

Four days before they were due to sail, Frank brought a guest with him to the Grant's dinner party held to honour Cecilly and Frank's engagement. Lucy had helped with the invitations, and despite the short notice, few guests had refused. Mr. William Marshall was introduced as an old friend of Frank's. Lucy guessed he was a few years older than Frank; however, he possessed the same liveliness as his friend. Perhaps all young Americans had a similar zest for life. She hoped so and looked forward to meeting many more of their kind in New York.

Marshall's blue eyes sparkled when he was introduced to her. She thought his manner too familiar, as he squeezed her hand tightly. And the way his eyes seemed to roam over her figure made her feel uncomfortable. She tore her gaze away. However, her escape was only temporary, as she sat next to him at dinner. Hardie couldn't have been further away. He sat at the opposite end of the table, next to Lady Grant.

Over dinner, she learned that Marshall had one overwhelming passion: aviation.

"Have you been flying recently?" Lucy asked.

"I've been touring in Europe and competing in air races."

"How adventurous! I remember following the *Daily Mail* Circuit of Britain Air Race last year. I was in France at the time, and the newspaper coverage was extensive."

He nodded. "Probably because it was won by a Frenchman. You're very well informed, Miss Mainwaring. Have you ever been flying?"

"No, but with so many flying machines being built, I'm sure it won't be long before we are all taking to the skies."

He laughed. "Indeed, if only that were so."

As he proceeded to tell her and those guests around him about his adventures, she couldn't help thinking how outgoing he sounded, almost to the point of conceit. Perhaps as an American he was less reserved than an Englishman. How different he was from Hardie. Yet, there was no doubt in her mind which man she preferred.

She stole a few glances along the table in Hardie's direction, but Lady Grant appeared to have him engaged in conversation. Cecily and Frank sat opposite each other in the middle of the table and seemed to have eyes for no one else. It pleased Lucy to see them so. She smiled at them, felt happy for them, and wished her situation could be as simple. Although nothing had been said to her, she found herself in an awkward position. If she did change her mind about Hardie, would *she* have to bring up the subject of marriage? And if so, how? Perhaps there would be opportunities to spend time together when they set sail, as her uncle had hinted.

* * * *

When Hardie heard Lady Grant summon the ladies to the drawing room, he rose with the gentlemen. As the ladies promenaded behind Lady Grant, he watched Lucy. He knew he was still smarting from her rebuff, but he only had himself to blame. His first approach, albeit an honest one, had been too abrupt. He claimed no great understanding of women, but had begun to admire aspects of Lucy's character. He liked her good sense, although her failure to acknowledge the danger she might be placing herself in caused him concern. The responsibility was his, he acknowledged, and his alone. Hadn't he placed her in jeopardy in the first place?

He twisted the stem of his port glass between his forefinger and thumb before downing the contents in one.

"Cigar, sir?" The butler at his elbow offered him a choice of the finest Havanas.

He declined and thought again about Lucy. He tried to see his proposal from her point of view. Her cool, clear logic forced him to admit she was right. His proposal had been founded on doing the *honourable thing* rather than concern for their future compatibility. But he felt responsible for her and the danger he had exposed her to. But he couldn't get her out of his head. He admired her composure, so different from her cousin and the many other young ladies he had met. He recalled the warmth of her lips, the delicate aroma of her subtle perfume, and the softness of her copper, rich hair. He was attracted to her. He admitted it, and he wanted to know her better, much better.

* * * *

Lucy had just refilled her coffee cup when the men joined the ladies in the drawing room. Sir Leyster drew her to one side. "Have you given the matter we discussed some thought?"

"Yes, Uncle Leyster, I have reconsidered." She stirred her coffee more vigorously than was necessary.

"And? What have you decided?"

"That you are probably right."

He smiled briefly. "Very wise. Get to know the man. He's a fine fellow. I think you'd better tell him now before you change your mind. Wait here, I'll send him over."

"But—" Her heart sank as she watched her uncle cross the room and tap Hardie on the shoulder.

He looked very distinctive in his best dress uniform. As he turned towards her, she thought she saw a slight smile hover on his lips. And as he approached, other people in the room seemed to fade into the background. A few seconds later, he was at her side, holding an empty cup.

"Would you like some more coffee?" Lucy asked.

"Thank you, if it is not too much trouble. I understand you are accompanying the family to America. Have you been to New York before?"

Lucy placed her own cup on the side table and picked up the coffee pot. It took all her control to stop her hand from shaking as she poured the warm liquid into his cup. "No, it will be my first trans-Atlantic crossing."

"It's a rare opportunity to sail on a ship's maiden voyage. Much has been written in the newspapers about White Star's new liner. Have you been following the articles?"

Glad to talk about the forthcoming voyage instead of marriage, Lucy felt some of her inner tension drain away. However, she wasn't sure if he was teasing her about reading the newspapers. "Of course I have."

"And what is your opinion of the new ship?"

"Lieutenant-Commander, I believe you are teasing me!"

He looked at her sheepishly, his full mouth breaking into a smile. "Whatever gave you that idea?"

"A serving navy officer and you ask for my views on a ship! I've only ever travelled on the cross-Channel ferry."

"Yes, but you do read the newspapers."

"True, but my knowledge is only secondhand. I have no personal experience. I know the *Titanic* is a huge vessel, because I have read a great deal about her. When I see her, I expect to be completely overwhelmed by her size."

"She is the largest vessel ever built."

"Indeed, I have also read that she is unsinkable."

Hardie shook his head. "Do not believe it. I doubt her designer, Mr. Andrews, would make such a claim. I understand he will be sailing with us, and he is very proud of his new ship."

"I am sure he has every right to be. I shall look forward to making his acquaintance and congratulating him on his work." Lucy glanced quickly around; she didn't want to be overheard. "I wish to speak to you about a certain matter. Perhaps we could walk towards the piano? Lady Grant has asked me to play."

"Do you sing as well?"

"Only in church."

He placed his empty coffee cup on the side table and escorted her the length of the room. When they reached the grand piano, she picked up the train of her gown and sat on the stool. "Sir Leyster asked me to reconsider your offer of marriage. Is that your wish too?"

"The circumstances remain. However, I would welcome the opportunity to know you better."

"So would I," she said as she played the opening bars of her favourite piece of Chopin.

* * * *

Two days before sailing, Lucy woke in the middle of the night. She had dreamt of wild, galloping horses, weird flying machines, and miles of ocean. To force the images from her mind, she thought of Hardie. She remembered his warm touch, strong embrace, and mellow voice. His presence gave her the greatest pleasure. She took comfort in the knowledge that he would protect her. Yet there was nothing protective about the deep sensations he aroused within her. Feelings she had never known before. Was she, like one of the heroines of the romances she had read, falling in love?

The question stunned her for a few moments. But then she became restless again. She turned one way and then the next. Eventually, she lay on her back and tried to focus her eyes on the ceiling. It was no use. She couldn't rest. Perhaps if she took a turn around the room, she would feel better. She eased herself out of bed and took a few paces towards the window.

A muffled thud coming from the street outside froze her to the spot. She listened carefully and thought she heard the rattle of window panes and wood sliding on wood coming from below. Had someone opened one of the sash windows below at street level? Standing as still as rock, she heard several more muffled sounds from the ground floor.

Tip-toeing to the window, she made a chink in the curtains and gazed at the empty square below. The street was deserted, but her restlessness wouldn't leave her. She slipped into her dressing gown and ventured onto the landing. Everything appeared to be in order downstairs in the hall, except for a light. It flickered inside Sir Leyster's study, the door of which, unusually, stood open.

Perhaps he was working on his speech for the peace conference? Instinctively Lucy felt something was wrong. She balanced her weight evenly on her feet and edged her way towards the lighted room. With each step she took a long, slow breath.

Footsteps, soft but purposeful, pinned her against the oak panelling as if she had been physically restrained. Then she saw him. A dark silhouette of a man framed in the doorway.

Silently she prayed he wouldn't see her, but when a thin shaft of moonlight fell across the hall from the skylight above, his masked face turned towards her. She gasped and tried to scream, but he leapt across the hall, seized her by her hair, and flung her backwards into the study. She crashed into something solid and sank to the floor. Terrified he was about to pounce on her, she crawled behind her uncle's desk and made herself as small as possible.

Long, anguished-filled minutes stretched out, until she realised she was alone. Slowly she emerged from her hiding place and took a few tentative steps. Moonlight flooded in from the hall, the lower shutters of the study window were flung wide, and a cool April breeze wafted into the house. Lucy stood in silence. *Arouse the household*, demanded an inner voice. She rushed into the hall, seized the hammer, and struck the dinner gong.

As she waited for the staff to respond, Hardie's image flashed before her. Why had she placed herself in danger once more? What had come over her? Why had she left her room in the middle of the night? Why had it fallen upon her to interrupt a burglar? She had acted foolishly and put herself at risk again. A chill crept through her bones and she shuddered.

* * * *

The following morning, Sir Leyster addressed the entire household in the drawing room. He outlined what had happened during the night and concluded, "Due to our forthcoming voyage, any valuables in the safe have been deposited in the bank vault. The police may question some of you later. This is routine procedure, so do not worry. To those deprived of sleep in the early hours of the morning, I thank you for your patience and loyalty."

After he dismissed the servants, he spoke to the family in private. "Unfortunate business, but it won't stop us sailing."

"Oh, thank you, Papa. I've been in a flutter. I thought we might not be going. What would Frank and I do?"

"I'm sure you would find a way to be together. However, I do not condone wandering around the house in the middle of the night. Lucy, it was brave of you to chase a thief, but very unwise. I don't want anything like this to happen again. Do you understand?"

"Yes, Uncle Leyster."

"I'm horrified when I think what could have befallen the girl." Lady Grant said.

"Yes, we understand." Sir Leyster took out his pocket watch, checked the time, and snapped the watch case shut.

"She could have been—"

"Maud, enough!"

There followed a few moments of unease. Lucy had never heard her uncle lose his temper with either his wife or daughter before. The silence was broken by a knock on the door.

The butler entered, carrying a salver. "Excuse me sir, there's a telegram for Miss Grant. It is marked urgent, sir."

"Very well, give it to her."

Lady Grant turned to her daughter. "Read it to us, dearest. If news of last night is about town, we must have a plan to limit the damage."

Cecilly tore open the envelope. "It's from Southampton, dated early this morning. 'Dearest Cecilly, Cable from New York. Father ill. Must return home on first available passage. Regret cannot sail with you. Will wait in New York. Impatiently. Your beloved Frank.' Oh! Mama! How could he do this to me?"

Lucy placed a comforting arm around her cousin's shoulders. "It'll only be a few days. We'll be in New York ourselves next week."

"But what fun can I have on board without him?" Cecilly pouted.

* * * *

Before luncheon, Lucy received a summons to her uncle's study where she expected to meet the police inspector. Instead, Hardie waited for her, alone.

"I persuaded Sir Leyster to occupy the inspector for a few moments. I hope you don't mind."

"If you're about to chastise me for my behaviour last night, then have your say and be done. It was stupid of me, but I was in the middle of it before I realised what was happening and—"

"Take care, Lucy," he cut in. "You could still be in danger."

"This isn't connected to the other incident, is it?"

"I hope not." He closed the distance between them. "Next time, please try to think before you act."

"Next time?"

"Yes, next time, because nothing I say seems to prevent you getting into some predicament or other. Your natural curiosity always seems to triumph over your good sense. By all means question, Lucy, but don't take unnecessary risks." A glimmer of a smile hovered on his lips. "And when are you going to start calling me Edwin?"

Chapter Six

"There's nothing like her afloat," Sir Leyster declared as the boat train steamed slowly through Terminus Station and halted beside the platform adjacent to the quay.

As they emerged from the carriage, Lucy felt a fresh breeze on her face and smelled the salty air of the Solent. The busy harbour surrounded by cranes, gantries, and sidings faded into oblivion on first sight of the gigantic ship berthed in the White Star Line Dock. Huge columns of greyish smoke drifted from her tall funnels. Amazed by her size, Lucy tilted her head right back to stare at the huge liner and nearly lost her hat. "It's like beholding one of the wonders of the modern world."

"She's colossal!" Cecilly gasped. "Exactly as Frank described her."

They boarded the ship via the first class gangway and were escorted to their staterooms. Whilst the servants unpacked, the girls went to the Boat Deck with Edwin. They waited for the moment the mighty ship got underway. Lucy clung to the ship's rail and marvelled at the crowd below. People waved, shouted, and cheered. A brass band played. At last, bells rang, heralding their departure. "She's off!" several voices around them cried.

The great engines began to turn as hats and caps were lifted aloft. Thousands of white handkerchiefs waved from an ocean of hands as the distant crowds bid farewell to the liner. A mighty cheer came from the nearby spectators and, spontaneously, the passengers replied almost in unison.

Lucy took a deep breath. She wanted to savour the moment. "Isn't this exciting, Cecilly? Our first trans-Atlantic crossing has begun."

"If only Frank was with us," she sighed.

"He will be in a few days. He'll be on the dock waiting for us to disembark. And we'll see the Statue of Liberty as we sail into New York. Look, Cecilly, at those men and boys running along the quay. They're trying to keep pace with us."

As the *Titanic* cleared the dock entrance, several loud bangs cracked in the air. "What was that?" Cecilly cried.

"Another vessel's moving towards us," Edwin answered.

Lucy grasped the ship's rail and cried, "We're going to collide!"

She grabbed Edwin's arm with her other hand. Huge coils of heavy rope flew through the air. The crowd on the quay scattered. Desperate cries came from the smaller vessel as she veered uncontrollably in the *Titanic's* direction.

Edwin covered her hand with his. "Don't worry, Captain Smith has stopped all engines."

Lucy peered over the ship's rail. Much to her relief they glided through the water and cleared the smaller ship with ease.

"Time for luncheon. The sea always gives me an appetite." Edwin offered an arm to each of the girls and escorted them to the first-class dining room. Inside, the ship's orchestra was playing a cheerful ragtime tune. They were shown to their table, where they found Sir Leyster and Lady Grant waiting for them. The table had been laid for six, as Frank had been originally included in Grant party.

"Mama, the most dreadful collision has nearly occurred." Cecilly sat down opposite her mother and proceeded to give her version of the incident.

Lucy remained silent throughout, although she thought Cecilly's account of the events somewhat exaggerated. She gave Edwin a glance across the table. He rewarded her with a knowing smile.

Lady Grant shook her head. "It's a bad omen. The very moment I found out we were sailing on this ship, I had a strange feeling about the whole affair. What sensible person sails voluntarily on a ship's maiden voyage?"

Sir Leyster gave his wife a cursory look. "This ship is the very latest design. It's a privilege to sail on her maiden voyage. It'll be something to tell your—" He stopped abruptly when William Marshall entered the dining room.

Boldly the young American strode towards the Grant's table, a wide grin on his face. "Good day, Sir Leyster, ladies, Hardie. I tried to catch up with your party sooner, but I had no idea of the size of this liner. I've been strolling around completely lost since I boarded."

Both Sir Leyster and Hardie stood up and shook Marshall's hand, the ladies remaining seated.

"Good afternoon, Mr. Marshall, and what a surprise. You gave no indication you would be making this crossing when we last saw you. When did you decide to take passage?" Sir Leyster asked.

"It was rather sudden. When I met Frank two days ago, I reminded him of a recent wager we had agreed upon. A fellow aviator down at Brooklands claimed he could lie on his back in the middle of Piccadilly amidst all the traffic for half an hour and not get hurt. Frank said he couldn't, but knowing the chap was a flyer, I had a notion he had some plan or other. You can imagine the look on Frank's face when he learned that the chap parked his automobile in the middle of the street and lay under it for the allotted time." Marshall's face broadened into a wide grin.

"I heard that story at my club the other day," Sir Leyster said. "Sopwith, that was the man's name. Do you know him?"

Marshall's face twitched. Lucy noticed it and wondered if the others did. "No sir, we're not acquainted, but I would like to meet him. Frank was worried about his father. As he left to board the next boat train to Southampton, he took something out of his pocket. 'Take this!' he shouted to me and jumped into a cab. He gave me his *Titanic* ticket in lieu of our wager, so here I am."

"That being the case, Mr. Marshall, perhaps you would care to join us?" Sir Leyster indicated the spare place at their table.

* * * *

After luncheon Lady Grant announced her wish to retire to her stateroom. Sir Leyster said he had a paper to write.

"Do you require my assistance, sir?" Edwin asked as they rose to leave.

"Not at all. I'm sure you'd much rather stay with Lucy and Cecilly. Why not explore the ship?"

"What a splendid idea, Papa."

"Do not tire yourself, Cecilly; we have already endured the train journey from London today." Lady Grant took her husband's arm and they left the dining room.

Cecilly turned to Marshall. "In the absence of my beloved Frank, as his friend you must escort me. And Hardie can squire Lucy."

"It would be an honour and a privilege. Fortunately I discovered I'd been given a White Star guide." He took the small book out of his top pocket and showed it to the other three. "This is how I found my way here. It's easy if you follow the plan and the illuminated signs around the ship. We must view the plunge pool," Marshall insisted as he led Cecilly on ahead.

It was the opportunity Lucy had been hoping for. "Edwin," she whispered, "something has bothered me since the burglary." He bent his head towards her as they slowed their pace. "Papers were stolen from the study that night. I know they were because I saw the thief with the folders. But when my uncle told the staff the safe had been empty, I didn't know what to say to the police inspector. Fortunately, he didn't ask. Surely my uncle knew what was in his own safe."

Edwin didn't reply immediately. "Have you asked him about this?"

"No, should I have mentioned it?"

"Documents were stolen. The police carried out their enquiries, but the real investigation is in the hands of another government department. It's all very secret." Anxiously he looked along the corridor. "I believe we are detaining our companions."

She followed his gaze the length of the passageway lined with stateroom doors. Cecily beckoned her from the far end.

"I believe my cousin is anxious for us to join them." She smiled up into Edwin's dark blue eyes. If only she knew how he felt about her. It could make so much difference to their relationship. Their voyage had hardly begun, yet she had no doubt about her overwhelming desire to be with him. If only their friendship could grow into love.

* * * *

Later that afternoon as the ship steamed towards Cherbourg, Lucy took tea with Lady Grant in her stateroom. Cecily had been excused. The excitement of the day, along with lunch had proven too much for her. She had taken to her bed, moaning she would never go to sea again. The task of watching over the patient fell to Cecilly's maid, Monique.

"Be vigilant." Lady Grant offered her niece a cup of tea.

Lucy frowned slightly and wondered if her aunt knew of Edwin's proposal. "In what manner?"

"Some Americans are too familiar. The ship is full of them. I've been over the first-class passenger list. There are dozens of people with whom we are not acquainted. And Americans think nothing of introducing themselves."

Inwardly Lucy breathed a sigh of relief. "I'm sure whilst Cecilly and I have the protection of Lieutenant-Commander Hardie and Mr. Marshall, it is unlikely we shall be approached by strangers."

"Hmm...I am not so easily convinced." She put her tea cup down with a slight rattle of the china. "You know I was against this voyage from the start, so I suppose I shall find fault at every turn. Call it a woman's intuition if you like. I'm sure you understand, Lucy. Unfortunately, men seldom do."

"Yes, Aunt." Lucy nodded respectfully. She knew her ladyship rarely let down the barriers of her strict behavioural code. Doubtless her upbringing had been a strict one, although sometimes, in Lucy's opinion, she indulged her only daughter too much. However, their meeting had convinced her of one essential fact; Lady Grant was ignorant of Edwin's declared intentions.

When sufficient time had elapsed, Lucy politely excused herself and made her way to the reading and writing room where she had an appointment.

* * * *

The large, well-furnished room decorated with potted palm plants was virtually empty. It didn't surprise her. There were far more interesting places to take one's leisure on the ship. She sat at one of the tables, determined to finish the letter to her father which she had begun earlier.

"Excuse me, Miss Mainwaring." Instantly she recognised the American voice over her shoulder.

She glanced up and gazed into Marshall's carefree face. His eyes appeared to widen as he looked at her. His warm smile told her he was pleased to see her. Unfortunately, he was not the man she had been expecting, and her heart sank.

"Miss Mainwaring, I'm sorry to disturb you but you look so serene sitting there writing."

"It's a letter to my father. I'm trying to get it finished to catch the mail at Queenstown tomorrow."

"Then please forgive my intrusion, but I was speaking from an artist's eye. Would you mind if I sketched you?" His gentle drawl had an inviting lilt. "You could carry on writing."

"I didn't know you were an artist, Mr. Marshall. I would have understood an interest in all things mechanical, even scientific, but art? You surprise me."

"My interest is strictly amateur, but art was my mistress before I discovered flying." He cast his gaze around her, as if searching for the best angle. "I like the way the afternoon sunlight catches your hair."

The way his eyes swept over her left her in no doubt his interest was more than an artistic one. She felt her cheeks pink. "I don't mind, as long as I can finish my letter. However, I am expecting someone."

He sat opposite her, opened his sketch pad, and began work immediately. It was her chance to observe him closely. His broad, workmanlike hands with short, fat fingers were not those of an artist. He wore his light brown hair cropped short, which further emphasized the roundness of his head. He was clean shaven except for his upper lip, which supported a thick moustache. His most distinguishing feature was his bright blue eyes.

She glanced at her fob watch. "Can I talk, or would you prefer me to continue writing?"

"Please carry on with your letter. You must not disappoint your father."

He gave her another adoring look which made her wish she hadn't spoken. She re-read her last few lines, but couldn't think of anything more to add. She glanced at her watch again.

"I've not intruded on your privacy, have I?"

"No, really. It's all right." She knew she sounded unconvincing. She dipped her pen into the ink well and held it poised to write. Then she realised she had her back to the entrance. How could she see Edwin when he came?

Marshall's observant eye moved quickly between subject and paper. "Do you like the sea?"

She shifted in her seat, glad of the diversion. "Yes, very much. The sea's powerful, and constantly changing. It's calm one moment and stormy the next. I admire the sea's ability to change and its refusal to be conquered."

"And what of man's attempts to master the seas by building ships like this?"

"Man's ability to conquer the sea is proven by his building larger and larger ships. But where will it all end?"

"Who knows?" He grinned. "I shall call my sketch *Lucy Being Philosophical.* Don't you approve of the titans, Miss Mainwaring?"

"I applaud the skill which built this ship, but I think it's foolish to underestimate the sea's power. The newspapers reported that the *Titanic* was unsinkable, but when I mentioned it to Hardie, he doubted the claim. So now I am inclined to believe any ship can sink, including this one."

"Better not let Captain Smith hear you say that, otherwise you might not get an invitation to dine at his table." He chuckled.

"To be excluded from the captain's table would greatly offend Lady Grant, but not me." She paused for the few moments, hoping Hardie would soon join her. They had arranged to view the coast of France together when the ship reached Cherbourg.

"Will you sit for me again? I'd love to capture the passion in your beautiful eyes."

Lucy swallowed hard. It was time to stop any romantic feeling he may be nurturing for her, before it developed further. "May I see?"

He turned the sketch towards her.

"You've flattered me far too much."

He shook his head. "True beauty is merely reflected here."

They were words Lucy didn't want to hear from him. "You are talented, Mr. Marshall."

"Sure," he shrugged, "but artistic talent doesn't buy aeroplanes. The future is the air, if only investors would realise it."

"And your family?"

"I'm an only son, who expected to take over my father's ship-building business. Alas, that was not to be as the yard went bust. However, it probably wouldn't have worked out as my father and I never did see eye to eye."

"How unfortunate. So you began in ship-building and now it's aviation. Won't you start up in business again? I thought America was the land of opportunity."

"And the streets of London are paved with gold," he scoffed. "I have plans to start my own aircraft factory, once I've secured sufficient backing. It was the reason I came to England. Frank's keen to come in with me, if he can persuade his father. But Johnson Senior is as tough as rawhide. I doubt if he'll give his approval, unless the old boy's so ill Frank takes over."

"I see." she murmured, convinced his interest in her would wane when he knew she was penniless. She glanced at her watch again.

"Looks like your friend isn't going to show."

"Show?"

"Sorry, an unfortunate turn of phrase. Perhaps he's not coming?"

A message boy in White Star uniform entered the room. "Paging Miss Mainwaring," he called.

Marshall waved him over. "This is Miss Mainwaring." He put his hand in his pocket and tipped the lad a few coins.

Lucy picked up the envelope from the silver salver offered to her. Instantly she recognised the precise hand of the sender, and her heart sank. She slit open the envelope using the letter opener from the desk and read the contents. Edwin wouldn't be coming and sent his apologies.

"Not bad news?"

"No." She put on a brave smile. "I was hoping the catch a last glimpse of France."

"Then, will you allow me to escort you on deck?" He asked, packing away his sketch pad and pencils in a brown leather satchel.

Lucy had misgivings. She didn't want to encourage his attentions, but if she could make him aware of her poor relation status in the Grant family, she felt sure his attentions would soon cease.

* * * *

"Look," Lucy cried, as she gazed through a window on the enclosed Promenade Deck, "the tenders are disembarking passengers. I wonder if they are going north or south?"

"Ah," Marshall sighed. "The south of France, Monte Carlo, Nice, Cannes...sandy coves, rocky headlands, white villas shaded by cypresses and olive groves. You never forget the colours, like the Garden of Eden. Do you know the Mediterranean coast well?"

"No, I've never been that far south."

He raised his eyebrows. "Really?"

This was the perfect opportunity to paint a clear picture about her financial prospects, and she intended to make good use of it. "I'm not part of the wealthy aristocracy."

"But Sir Leyster—"

"Is my uncle and Cecilly's the heiress, not me. I'm the poor relation up from the country. My father does not have the means to finance travel to the south of France."

He paused for a few moments. "But you've got something New York society hasn't."

She looked at him quizzically. "And that is?"

"Connections, Miss Mainwaring. However tenuous they are, I guarantee within a week you'll be the toast of the town."

"Mr. Marshall, you are discovered! Not only is your artwork sheer flattery, but also your words."

A guilty look flashed across his face. Then he burst into a fit of laughter which gladdened Lucy's heart. Their conversation had not become too serious and, hopefully, his attentiveness would soon cease. Taking his arm they continued along the enclosed deck and ascended to the Boat Deck. Together they watched the dusk descending rapidly in the western sky. They stood in silence and witnessed the last of the third class passengers embarking. They were mainly migrants quitting the Old World, bound for the New.

Chapter Seven

"Are you sure you can't manage dinner?" The black look accompanied by Cecilly's loud groan answered Lucy's question. "Monique, has the doctor called?"

"Her ladyship spoke to him an hour ago, Miss."

"What did he say?" Lucy asked?

"I've got sea malady. At least Frank can't see me like this."

"I'm sure you'll feel better tomorrow." Lucy took her cousin's hand in hers and gently patted it. "We've left the French coast, and we'll be off southern Ireland tomorrow morning."

"Oh...why do I feel so ill? I'm dying...I've never felt so ill in my life."

"Do you want me to stay with you?"

"No...you must go to dinner. Ugh! The thought of food."

With Monique's help, Lucy dressed in one of Cecilly's rejected gowns. She wasn't used to the low-cut bodice and stared at herself in the mirror. As the skirt narrowed at the bottom, she would have to remember to take short steps. Finally, Monique added a matching blue feather to the bandeau in Lucy's hair.

From her bed, Cecilly nodded her approval. "Blue is a good colour for you. It suits your flaming red hair."

Lucy patted the large bun which Monique had arranged. She hoped wiry tendrils didn't escape before the end of the evening.

Cecilly beckoned her closer. "This trip will be your last chance with Hardie," she whispered, "or do you prefer the American?"

Lucy glared back and tried to dismiss the remarks with the contempt they deserved. But she felt her cheeks growing hotter. Cecilly blinked and tried to smile. Her face was very pale snuggled against the eiderdown.

* * * *

Sir Leyster escorted his wife and niece to their table in the dining room where they were joined by Marshall. When the American sat next to Lucy without invitation, Lady Grant shot her a warning look. It was obvious her ladyship disapproved of the young man's forwardness.

With no further word from Edwin since his note in the late afternoon, Lucy felt disappointed. Since they had reached an agreement about reconsidering their match, she had expected to spend some time in his company. Could he be having second thoughts?

Her anxiety evaporated when the man closest to her heart entered the dining room. He looked resplendent in formal evening dress. She caught her breath as her heart began to quicken. The flash of his dark eyes as he greeted her sent a surge of sheer joy through her veins. She smiled and bathed inwardly in the knowledge she was falling in love with him.

Edwin took the seat next to Lady Grant, which placed him directly opposite Marshall and Lucy. The table conversation drifted on about the ship and her luxury fittings. Once more, Lady Grant expressed her uneasiness about the voyage. However, Lucy noticed how Sir Leyster tactfully silenced his wife with a single stern look. She wondered if the gentlemen noticed too.

"Have you been up on the bridge?" Sir Leyster addressed Edwin.

Lucy felt ashamed. It hadn't occurred to her that he might have spent the afternoon with the captain and his officers. She chastised herself inwardly for being so selfish.

"Yes, I have, sir. Not the same as the Dreadnought class, of course, but she's a mighty ship. There are only a few berths big enough to take her."

"Is that why tenders were used at Cherbourg?" Lucy asked.

"Absolutely!" Edwin paused to smile at her. "They'll be used again tomorrow at Queenstown." He turned to speak to the whole table. "Captain Smith runs a tight ship; everything is well in hand. He has every right to feel proud. She's a fine vessel."

"Have you been below decks?"

"Aye, Marshall, I have. Second Officer Lightoller took me below. The engine room is perfection. As passengers we see only a small amount of the ship. Her internal corridors, galleys, and storage facilities are something to behold. Lightoller's a good guide. He knows the ship inside out. No mean feat, when you consider she's the biggest afloat."

"Do you think this fellow would take me round?" Marshall asked.

"Make a request to the bridge."

"Is she all they claim?" Again, Marshall addressed Edwin and ignored his other table companions.

"In what respect?"

"The hull, the watertight doors, bulkheads, and the like. Is she sound? And the accommodation; we've seen first, but what are second and third like?"

Edwin paused and gave Lucy a slight glance. "If you're concerned about the structure, I suggest you speak to Mr. Andrews, the designer. He's on board. As for those passengers travelling in second and third, why not make your own enquiries?"

"There speaks a budding diplomat, don't you think?" Sir Leyster chuckled.

"Diplomat?" Marshall echoed. "Have you ambition in that direction? I thought you were a serving officer, Hardie."

"I am, but perhaps another career might tempt me in the future, who knows?"

Throughout dinner, the table conversation switched to other topics. These included the Marconi service and the daily news bulletins. Much to Lucy's annoyance, news items were posted in the gentleman's smoke room, where ladies were not received.

After dinner, they went to hear the concert performed by the ship's orchestra on A Deck. Quickly Lucy realised entertainment in first-class served a two-fold purpose—to see and be seen. In his brash, American way, Marshall didn't hesitate to point out to her some of the more important guests.

"That's Mrs. J.J. Brown over there." He indicated a middle-aged matron of generous proportions. "J.J. struck it rich in the gold mines in '94. She's a very rich widow. Shunned by Denver society, she travels the world, entertains extravagantly, and has recently been in Egypt with the Astors. She embarked today with them. Everyone calls her Molly."

Alas, the extremely wealthy John Jacob Astor IV and his new wife Madeleine were not to be seen. Lucy made a mental note of the fact to report back to Cecilly, who might take consolation in not having missed them. For her own part, she didn't care.

When the concert finished, she had the unaccustomed luxury of two gentlemen in close attendance. They drifted towards their rooms. Somewhat formally, she bade each man goodnight and tapped on her door. Monique answered, and she slipped inside and found Cecilly asleep.

A few minutes later there was a soft knock on the door.

"I'll answer that," she told the maid. Outside she found Edwin, looking at her with doleful eyes.

"Can we talk?" His voice was hushed, as he glanced both ways along the corridor. "Perhaps we could take a stroll on deck."

"I'll get my coat and scarf," Lucy whispered.

He nodded.

She asked Monique for her outdoor coat, as if there was nothing unusual about going on deck alone with a gentleman at a late hour. "Wait with Miss Cecilly until I return." She slipped into the heavy, woollen coat and threw the scarf around her head and shoulders. Outside in the stateroom, she took Edwin's arm and allowed him to escort her along the corridor. Inwardly she prayed her aunt wouldn't spot them together.

He led her up to the Promenade Deck. It was fairly crowded with couples taking a final stroll before turning in for the night. "Let's go up to the Boat Deck," he suggested. "Will you be warm enough?"

She nodded. "I think so."

As they emerged into the cold evening air, her first thoughts were for him. "Won't you be cold? You've no top coat."

"Don't worry, I'll survive."

The Boat Deck, now devoid of people, looked huge compared to their last visit when it had been filled with passengers waving goodbye to their home port. Edwin led her to the first-class port side, where they sheltered from the sharp evening air in the shadow of a lifeboat.

"I'm sorry I couldn't keep our appointment this afternoon. I heard you spent time with Marshall?"

She detected censure in his voice and felt the need to explain herself. "He wanted to sketch me. He's a talented artist."

"I'm sure his interest stretches further than an artistic one." He squeezed her hand gently as he spoke. "Be careful, Lucy, the man's a gold-digger."

"Then he's not likely to waste time with me. If he's after money, there's plenty on board. Perhaps he ought to pay court to Mrs. Brown."

"Lucy," he implored closing the space between them. "You can tell him you're as poor as a church mouse, but you're closely related to the Grants. An unscrupulous man wouldn't hesitate to use the connection to his advantage." Her mouth dropped open as he pulled her towards him. "Believe me, Lucy, Marshall's up to no good."

She wanted to reply, but knew the time for words had passed. She titled her head upwards, ready to receive his lips. Her body melted against his. It was their first real kiss. She wanted to savour the touch of his warm lips on hers. No longer used as a charade to fool a spy, the silky softness of his mouth proved enticing. She wanted more.

Tingling sensations coursed through her veins. The strength of his arms secured her to his sturdy, male frame. If only the world could stay in this moment forever, she would be perfectly content.

When the kiss broke, she looked up into his dark eyes. The yellowish glow of the ship's electric system softened his skin tone. His dark, wavy hair, slightly tousled, made her want to run her fingers through it. She inhaled the enticing aroma of his newly shaven jaw. *I love this man*, she breathed in silently, *if only he could love me.*

He kissed her neck and the soft, sensitive skin behind her ears. There they remained for several moments, in each other's embrace. Only the constant drone of the ship's engines rang in their ears as the *Titanic* steamed her way to the Irish coast.

"Edwin, I couldn't stop Marshall drawing me this afternoon. I was writing to my father. And when I mentioned the Cherbourg embarkation, he offered to escort me. You don't like him, do you?" She gazed into his eyes, trying to read his thoughts. She trusted him implicitly and believed he would tell her the truth.

"Whether I like him or not is immaterial. I promised Sir Leyster I would look out for you. I don't want to see you deceived or hurt."

Lucy's heart sank. Again he was acting out of duty. "How can—"

"Someone's coming." He pulled her further under the shadow of the lifeboat.

Pressed tightly against his chest, she felt secure and protected in the darkness. But as footsteps approached, she could feel her heart pounding rapidly. It could be anyone—a fellow passenger, a steward, a crewman, an officer. Whoever it was halted. Lucy heard a match being struck, and a few moments later, smelt the pungent aroma of a cheroot.

The burning tobacco tinged the air, and Lucy tried to close her nostrils to avoid breathing it in. Standing alone with Edwin, his arms around her, she tried to pretend the intruder, only a few feet from them, didn't exist. Her stomach turned over and sent the bitter taste of bile surging into her mouth. The cheroot was the same as the one smoked in the conservatory the night of the embassy ball. For one dreadful instant, she thought she might faint.

She felt Edwin's forefinger on her lips, signalling her to keep still. She held on to him tightly, through what seemed a great abyss of time. In truth, it could only have been a few seconds. The ship's engines droned on.

Straining her ears, she heard the footsteps retreat. "Has he gone?"

"I think so." He released her and together they emerged from their hiding place. "This is becoming a habit."

Lucy shivered. "I was so scared...that cheroot...I swear it smelled the same as..." She trailed off, unable to bring herself to speak the name of a man she feared.

"Merely a coincidence. There must be many men aboard smoking similar brands. You must be cold. We should go back."

Lucy took Edwin's arm, and they strolled to the top of the stairs leading to their staterooms on B Deck. But they halted abruptly when they saw the man smoking the cheroot. He swept aside his caped coat and placed his gold watch into the pocket of his waistcoat.

Stunned, Lucy froze as fear gripped the pit of her stomach. The man looked at them but didn't wait for any acknowledgement. He turned his back, pulled up his collar, and skulked away like a wounded beast from a fight. Lucy's hand flew to her mouth. She let out a loud gasp and buried her face in Edwin's shoulder. "Why is he here?"

"I don't know," he answered. "Promise me you'll stay inside your stateroom and don't venture out alone under any circumstances. I'll report to your uncle immediately."

* * * *

As Edwin knocked on the Grant's door, he hoped his superior had not retired. Sir Leyster, still dressed, answered.

"Forgive the intrusion, sir, but an urgent matter has arisen," Hardie said.

Sir Leyster gave him a quizzical look. "Your stateroom?"

Edwin nodded and led the way along the corridor. He waited until they were inside and the door firmly closed before speaking to Sir Leyster. "The Comte D'Every is on board. Lucy and I saw him less than ten minutes ago."

"Good God, man! Do you realise what this could mean?"

"That Lucy and I could be in danger?"

Sir Leyster scratched his head. "But why pursue either of you? I don't understand, unless the man is obsessed with twisted revenge."

"He runs a professional spy ring. He hasn't got time for revenge."

"But he is ruthless. How else can he keep his underlings in check? They fear him and what revenge he might mete out on them if they betray him. The man's a master of deception, cruelty, and sheer bloody-mindedness."

Edwin thought for a few moments. "When we saw him, one thing troubled me. He seemed as surprised to see us as we were to confront him. I'd almost believe we met accidentally."

"So, why is he on board?"

"I don't know. The documents his accomplice stole from the embassy would have been disposed of by now. And if we believe he was responsible for the theft of our plans, why sail on a British ship? It doesn't make sense."

Sir Leyster shrugged. "Can I have some of your scotch?" He picked up the bottle of malt whisky from the side table, poured two glasses, and offered one to Edwin. "Perhaps our plans were stolen by another cohort. As for us being aboard, he only had to read the first-class passenger list, if he had access to it."

"Which might indicate he's travelling in second or even third." Edwin took a gulp of the whisky. "Let's assume he is travelling incognito, probably under an assumed name and in second class as he had access to the Boat Deck. Perhaps Lucy and I aren't his target anymore."

Sir Leyster shook his head. "That's all very well, but we can't be sure."

Edwin agreed. "He's already spread enough malicious rumours around London about me to blacken the character of a saint. I very nearly missed the ship because I had to explain myself to my father."

"I'm surprised the gossip went that far."

"My father may keep to his estate of late, but he maintains his contacts in town."

Sir Leyster downed his drink in one. "So what did he say?"

"He took great pains to remind me of my duty. He named her and claimed I had only one honourable course of action open to me. He refused to hear my account and said how fortunate I was not to have been shot on sight by your good self."

"Edwin, you need another drink." Sir Leyster refilled their glasses. "I know you haven't compromised Lucy."

Edwin accepted the second scotch and was about to drink it when his temper flared. "Damnation, I've injured her reputation nevertheless. The fault is mine, and mine alone."

"It is not. The Comte D'Every has done that. It is obvious he is the source. No self-respecting gentleman would allow himself to sink so low. To imply you violated a young lady's innocence in the conservatory of an embassy is slander enough. But to name the young lady! He must have a vile disposition."

"I should not have taken her there in the first place. Then his lies would have no foundation."

"Don't carry on beating yourself."

Edwin noted the kindness in his superior's tone. "Lucy is too nice a young lady to be used like this." He downed his shot of whisky in one and Sir Leyster followed suit.

"We've got to find him," Sir Leyster stressed. "I'll brief Captain Smith in the morning. Do you and Lucy want to disembark at Queenstown?"

Edwin took a deep breath. "What purpose would running away serve? If we are targets of the comte's revenge, I'd rather face him here, where he can't escape. He could follow us in Ireland, or wherever we go. I would prefer to remain on board."

"And Lucy?"

"I believe she would too."

"And how are you two getting along?" A smile hovered around Sir Leyster's lips.

"Err...better I hope."

"She's a sensible girl, as you've no doubt discovered. However, she has a woman's passion, like her mother..." His voice trailed off and he stared blankly into the bottom of his empty whisky glass. "She needs to feel she's wanted. She deserves to be loved."

Chapter Eight

The next morning, as the *Titanic* sighted the Irish coast, Lucy remained in her stateroom. Monique had helped her dress and was adding the finishing touches to her hair, when Cecilly opened her eyes and groaned.

"How are you feeling, a little better?" Lucy asked.

Cecilly rubbed her eyes, took a deep breath, and sighed. "I've never felt so ill in my life."

"You might feel better when you've had some fresh air."

"Fresh air? You don't understand. I'm on death's door."

"Really Cecilly, you can't be as bad as that. I'm sure if Frank were here instead of me, you'd be restored in a flash."

Cecilly pouted. "I suppose so...perhaps I'll try to get up this afternoon."

Lucy went to the window. "It looks bright and sunny outside. Maybe we could go for a walk later?"

"I'm ill, I'm staying in bed."

Lucy glanced over her shoulder, as Monique straightened Cecilly's sheets and tucked in the blankets. It would be unwise to confide last night's events to Cecilly in her present condition. There was little to be gained by telling her they thought they had seen the Comte D'Every. The more Lucy thought about it, the more she tried to convince herself she had been mistaken. But Edwin had been with her. He had seen him too.

There was a knock on the door, which Monique answered. Lady Grant entered, accompanied by the ship's doctor.

"There's no need for you to stay Lucy," Lady Grant said. "Hardie is outside, and he wants to know if you'd care to watch the embarkation."

"That would be very pleasant indeed. My coat and hat please, Monique."

Suitably dressed, Lucy left. Not only was she relieved to get out of the confines of the stateroom, but she was also delighted to see Edwin waiting for her in the corridor. She took his arm. "Any news?"

"About our fellow traveller?" He shook his head. "He's not on any of the passenger lists."

"So he's travelling incognito?"

"That's not unusual for him. He's a man of many disguises."

As they approached the stairs, Lucy gripped Edwin's arm a little tighter. "Why is he here? Is he following us? For the first time in my life, I'm scared of another human being."

Edwin stopped and turned towards her, compassion in his eyes. "If I could change what happened that night in the conservatory, I would. The last thing I want is to see you hurt."

"Please don't blame yourself, Edwin."

"Who else should I blame? The man is a villain, he'll—"

111

"Then he *has* come after us?"

"No, I've discussed this with Sir Leyster. We believe it was a chance meeting. Remember, Lucy, he looked shocked to see us. If he was following us, he'd hardly risk tipping us off beforehand, would he?"

"I hope you're right." She squeezed his arm.

"Nevertheless, we must be vigilant. However, let's not deny ourselves a last look at land, eh?"

She didn't reply, but his words seemed to echo forebodingly through her, and a cold shiver crept along her backbone.

* * * *

The view from the Boat Deck revived Lucy. "I've not seen Ireland before," she said as she gazed at the green, rounded slopes and rugged cliff outcrops. "I didn't imagine the coastline would be so rugged."

"Can you see that fort to the east of the harbour entrance?" Edwin asked. "Captain Smith will use it as a reference point. And can you feel the ship's engines slowing?"

"Yes, and what is that small vessel approaching? It doesn't look like a tug."

Edwin shook his head. "She's carrying our pilot. He'll pull alongside and hop on board in a few minutes."

"But why do we need a pilot? I thought they were using the tenders to ferry passengers, like they did at Cherbourg."

"They will, but a pilot knows the local waters. The *Titanic's* too big to get into Queenstown, but the captain can't risk running aground. Under the pilot's orders he'll steam slowly, round the lighthouse, and probably drop anchor over there." Edwin pointed across the bay.

"How far are we from the mainland?"

"Under two miles."

They watched from the Boat Deck as the giant ship edged towards her anchorage. Breathing in the crisp air, Lucy felt very safe with Edwin at her side, and her hands linked around his arm. Several other passengers joined them on the first-class section of the Boat Deck as the tenders approached from the shore.

As the Irish passengers embarked, Lucy gazed down at the tiny figures, well-wrapped in thick clothing. The women pulled huge shawls about their shoulders; many had children and carried babies with them. Her eyes lingered on the youths—they looked so young. Her ears burnt with excitement. There was something special about this whole adventure. A gust of wind came from nowhere and nearly blew off her wide-brimmed hat. She had to let go of Edwin's arm and hold the hat to her head.

Edwin nudged her. "Look, Captain Smith's over there." He pointed to a stretch of deck where a group of officers stood, posing for press photographers.

Up on tip-toe Lucy craned to see over the gathering crowd. Captain Smith walked towards them accompanied by a motley crew of journalists, who jostled for the prime places alongside his rotund form. He strode proudly along the deck, leading the pressmen around his new flagship like the Pied Piper.

Lucy tingled with excitement. "Next stop, New York."

"Excited?"

"Yes, I'm trying to imagine the razzle-dazzle of the New World. The lights, the buildings, the people, the...oh...everything!"

* * * *

Shortly before they upped anchor, Lucy leaned over the ship's rail and noticed a fleet of small boats alongside the ship. "What are they doing?"

Edwin, too, leaned over the rail "Traders, I believe. A few will be allowed on board with their goods. The women sell linens, laces, embroidery, and Irish souvenirs. Would you like to view their wares?"

"Yes, very much." Lucy replied, then she remembered she had no money. She bit her lower lip. How could she tell Edwin she had spent all her savings on her wardrobe when she came to London? At the time, she had hoped her father might provide some extra funds. But he hadn't, and she was too proud to ask him. Together they strolled to where tables had been set up as makeshift market stalls.

"This work is beautiful." She pointed to a lace collar made of intricate layers of crochet flowers set in a delicate mesh and knew it would go well on her navy winter dress.

"Five shilling," the Irish woman said.

"Five shillings!" Lucy shook her head and moved away.

"Would you like the lace?" Edwin asked.

"It's far too expensive."

"But you would like it. I'll get it for you."

"No, I couldn't accept it. Really I can't."

His face creased. "Why not?"

"It's not that—" Her mouth dropped open as Marshall appeared at her elbow.

"Sure is a fine day for flying." He rubbed his hands together. "I saw you admiring the lace, Miss Mainwaring. Do you intend to purchase some?"

Her cheeks flushed. "It's all very lovely, but I don't think I will."

"Pity," he sighed, "Irish lace will be all the fashion now the Astors have bought some."

"Are they here?" Lucy looked around.

"Sure, right over there." He pointed to a well-dressed middle-aged gentleman and a very young lady standing arm in arm.

Lucy observed them both, knowing Cecily would want to know all about the famous couple.

"Coffee?" Marshall asked as they strolled away from the Irish pedlars. Lucy looked at Edwin.

"What an excellent idea," he replied.

Lucy hoped she had warned Marshall off from any further amorous intentions he might have towards her. Edwin had dubbed him a fortune-hunter, which she had accepted based on what she had learned of his character. He possessed a certain type of brashness that sometimes offended English reserve. Yet his character intrigued her. He had vitality, as if he burned up his life's energy at a faster rate than his staid contemporaries. His zest for life and his insatiable quest for adventure guaranteed he would travel great distances. He was a risk-taker, who laughed in the face of danger.

When they entered the Verandah Cafe, they were surprised to find the Grants there.

Sir Leyster beckoned them over to his table. "Lucy, my dear, I thought we might find you here. I'm afraid your aunt has had a shock."

Lucy sank onto the seat next to Lady Grant. "Is it Cecily? Is she worse?"

"Not at all." Sir Leyster resumed his seat. "Dr. O'Loughlin's convinced there's nothing the matter with her."

"Then what is wrong? Aunt Maud, can I help?"

Lady Grant took in a deep breath. "I wish I had never set foot on board this ship, but Sir Leyster persuaded me to take a turn on deck. I had a yearning to see land again. Albeit the coast of Ireland. My husband was pointing out certain aspects of the ship's structure when the ugliest face I have ever beheld shot up from inside one of those round shafts. I thought it was the devil himself."

Sir Leyster began to chuckle. "It was a stoker, giving the cowl vent a quick polish."

"A quick polish, indeed!" Lady Grant snapped. "You may laugh, but crew frightening the life out of passengers does not augur well for a ship. It's a bad omen."

"He's one of the black gang, a greaser. How can an ordinary working man be a bad omen?" Sir Leyster asked.

"I am sensitive to these matters," she declared firmly. "And I wasn't the only lady distressed by the sight of him. He ought to be dismissed at once. If he were a member of my staff I would—"

Sir Leyster's brow creased into a frown. "Enough, Maud, these young folk don't want to hear prophetic tales of doom and gloom."

"Aunt Maud, I'm so sorry the man upset you. But I'm sure he had no intention of doing so. As for his dismissal, he probably has a wife and family dependent upon him in Southampton."

"Lucy," Lady Grant said, "you have a kindly nature and you're always optimistic. But I have a more sensitive disposition. There is something about this ship that causes me great unease and what happened today has only reinforced my opinion."

Lucy wanted to say something but couldn't think of the right words to appease her aunt. It pleased her when Edwin leaned forward after a few silent moments.

"I have spent the greater part of my naval career at sea," he said, "and have come to appreciate how superstitious the ocean can make even hearty seamen. I have witnessed experienced sailors quake at the sight of an albatross."

Sir Leyster smiled as the waiter arrived with the coffee. "And I have witnessed much comfort derived from a pot of coffee."

* * * *

Realising her cousin must be feeling lonely Lucy took luncheon in their stateroom, although Cecilly didn't eat anything. Afterwards Lucy read to her until Dr. O'Loughlin, accompanied by Lady Grant, arrived at four o'clock.

"You must try to get up, Miss Grant," he urged. "I heartily recommend fresh air for sea malady."

Cecilly groaned. "I want to stay in bed."

The doctor shook his head and turned to Lady Grant. "Thirty years in the medical profession and I do not understand young women. I've done all I can today, Lady Grant. Not everyone takes to the sea. I hope the medicine I have prescribed will help Miss Grant."

"Thank you, doctor, you have been most attentive." Lady Grant left the stateroom soon after the doctor had quit.

"Please read some more of the novel, Lucy. You make it sound so real. I pretend I'm the heroine. I must know how I escape from the castle," Cecilly said.

Lucy opened the book and read until they were interrupted by a knock on the door. Monique answered. "The stewardess brought a package for you, Miss Mainwaring, and a note." She handed them both to Lucy.

Cecilly pushed herself up on her elbows and flicked her blonde hair off her face. "What's that?"

"I don't know," Lucy said, but she recognised the copper-plate handwriting on the envelope. Fingers shaking, she opened the letter first and read it.

"What does it say?" Cecilly asked.

"Edwin wants to talk to me later tonight." She peered impishly over the thick paper. "Alone."

"Oooow!" Cecilly's eyes widened. She looked better than she had done for two days.

"Would it be proper to go?" Lucy asked, feigning innocence.

"Of course it's not proper. But you'd be a fool not to!"

Pleased that some of Cecilly's former sparkle had returned, Lucy released the silk ribbon around the parcel and opened the paper. Wrapped inside was the crocheted collar she had admired. "There's no card."

"Must be from Edwin." Cecilly sank back into her pillows.

Lucy tried the collar against the lavender dress she was wearing. "It looks very well, but I have a better idea." She removed her favourite winter dress from the wardrobe, opened her sewing case, and picked up a needle and thread. Deftly, she began to attach the handmade lace to her dark blue gown.

* * * *

"I've invited a couple of guests to dine with us this evening," Sir Leyster said when they arrived at their table in the dining room. Two gentlemen approached, chatting to each other as they made their way towards the Grant party.

"My dear, you are already acquainted with Dr. O'Loughlin, but let me introduced Mr. Thomas Andrews, designer of the *Titanic.*"

"It's a privilege to make the acquaintance Mr. Andrews," Lady Grant said. "This is our niece, Miss Mainwaring, unfortunately our daughter is unwell and unable to dine this evening."

Shortly after they were seated, Marshall arrived. He didn't wait for a formal introduction. He shook Andrews's hand and took the place adjacent to him. "Mr. Andrews," Marshall said, "I'm delighted to meet you. It is an honour, sir, to dine with Harland & Wolff's Chief Designer."

When Edwin joined them, Lucy's stomach tensed. She hoped her excitement wouldn't be noticed by the others. If her dinner companions remarked about her newly acquired radiance, she would say it was the bracing sea air. Walks on the Boat Deck were very beneficial to one's health, she would tell them. Only she would know Edwin's company had more to do with her recent bloom.

Dinner conversation drifted from the ship, to Ireland, through to New York, and back to shipbuilding. Marshall and Andrews dominated the conversation, especially when technical matters were being discussed. Therefore, Lucy wasn't surprised that when the ship's designer rose to leave Marshall got to his feet as well and said, "It would be an enormous privilege to view your charts and drawings, sir."

Andrews nodded, thanked his host, bade farewell to the dinner party, and left with Marshall.

"Andrews lives, eats, and breathes this ship." The doctor explained after the pair had gone. "It's been his life blood since well before her keel was laid down. He's watched her grow like a father watches his child develop."

After dinner, the Grants made their way to the first-class lounge.

"It's somewhat crowded in here," Lady Grant complained, "and I haven't had a wink of sleep since I came on board."

"Of course, my dear, would you prefer to retire?" Sir Leyster offered his wife his arm.

"Sir, may I escort Miss Mainwaring to the Palm Court to take coffee?" Hardie asked.

"Capital idea, I understand it's becoming a favourite after-dinner haunt for you younger set. I'll accompany her ladyship back to our stateroom, then I'm for the smoking room."

The touch of Edwin's male hand as he tucked hers into the crook of his arm gave Lucy a warm, comforting feeling. She knew she was safe and secure when she was with him. They sat at a small table and ordered a pot of coffee. Whilst they waited, she took the opportunity to thank him for his gift.

"Gift?" His brow creased. "I don't understand."

Lucy felt the colour drain from her cheeks. "The lace collar that came with your note."

"I sent no lace," he told her flatly. "You said you couldn't accept it."

Her mouth dropped open. Mistakenly she had thought the gift had been the first tangible sign of his growing affection for her. Her heart had raced ahead of her reason. A few moments ago she was prepared to declare her love for him and accept his proposal. Now she was confused and turned away.

"Marshall was on hand," he said softly. "Please look at me, Lucy."

Heat flared in her cheeks as she turned towards him.

"Be careful, he's a philanderer," Hardie said.

"Yesterday he was a gold-digger, now a philanderer. What will he be tomorrow?"

A muscle flickered at the side of his face. "I've been checking up on Mr. William Marshall—"

"Spying on him?" She cut in then dropped her head. When she looked up at him again he was staring at her. "I'm sorry, Edwin, but I think you're wrong."

"Am I? Didn't you see how he forced himself upon Andrews earlier? I'm convinced he's up to no good."

She shrugged. "He's interested in ships. What's wrong with that? His father owned a shipyard before he went—"

"He told you that?" He let out a long sigh. "His mother and father were in vaudeville. He was brought up on the stage. For several years he has wandered around Europe living off rich women and gambling to finance his passion for flying. He's a first-class pilot, which is possibly the only genuine fact about the man."

Lucy's heart sank. Although she didn't consider Marshall a potential suitor, she had come to like him. "I'm sorry, I had no idea. I should have listened to you, but he seemed very amiable. I'll return the lace in the morning, but is there any news about…" she hesitated, half-afraid of what his answer might be. "The comte?"

He shook his head. "We've looked everywhere. It's as if the blackguard has vanished into thin air."

"Monique didn't find out anything either."

"Monique, what the devil have you told her?"

"Nothing! I described him, that's all. And…she asked around for a man fitting his description in the servant's lounge. Very little is missed there." She sensed his anger mounting, and her throat dried.

"That's the very way to draw attention to us. Servants gossip. Before you know it, word will get to him. Whatever were you thinking of?"

"I was only trying to help." Realising she had begun to annoy him, she stood up, scraping her chair on the floor. Several people turned around at the sound. Embarrassed, she rushed out.

As his footsteps were close behind her, she quickened her pace. "Confound this skirt!" she cried and hitched up the train.

He grabbed her hand and pulled her towards him. "Forgive me," he murmured his breath hot on her face, and his lips only inches from hers. "I have a confession to make. Let's walk."

Lucy struggled to keep pace with him. How could he annoy her one minute and a second later pluck at her heart strings?

He led her along the sheltered Promenade Deck until he found a secluded corner and stopped. Slipping his arms around her waist, he said, "A man fitting the comte's description embarked at Cherbourg. He's in Second Class but not in his cabin. I've spoken to his steward, but he hasn't seen the comte since he boarded."

She liked the strength of his arms around her but also felt the tension in his voice. "Is he hiding somewhere? Was our meeting him coincidental?"

"Obviously he doesn't want to be seen publically. As to our seeing him, I'm convinced of it. He beat a hasty retreat when he saw us and looked very surprised. He may be dangerous now he knows we are here. Whatever business brought him on this voyage, he's astute enough to use a chance meeting for his own ends."

As he drew her closer, she brought her hands up to rest on his chest. "Edwin, I am so pleased we are together. Knowing you are close helps, but I am still very worried."

"Dear Lucy, you have every right to be troubled knowing a man like the comte is close by."

"You said you thought our meeting with him was coincidental. If that is so, why is he going to New York?"

"Why is anyone?" He shrugged. "Over two thousand people are on this ship, probably all with their own reasons for making the crossing."

"What are we going to do?"

"Nothing initially, but please, Lucy, do as I ask."

In her heart she knew he was right. She trusted him implicitly and nodded her agreement. "Very well, Edwin, I will try to be cautious."

He smoothed a stray tendril of hair away from her face. "Let him make the first move. But make sure you are never alone. Don't open your door to anyone without identification. Once a voyage is underway, the stewards and stewardesses do not change. Don't answer your door to anyone save your regular women."

"I understand."

Initially they had been the only couple walking on the Promenade Deck, but now several others strolled towards them. Edwin glanced at the first couple who was only a few yards away. "Let's go up to the Boat Deck."

Lucy nodded, and hand in hand they climbed the stairs. As they emerged on the open deck a blast of cold air hit them and Lucy shivered.

"Take this," he removed his evening coat and wrapped it around her shoulders.

"There's no moon." She gazed up into the dark sky at thousands of twinkling stars defying the night like jewels on black velvet. They stood against the ship's rail and listened to the soft hum of the engines driving the giantess through the calm sea.

"Lucy." He said her name slowly as if he had difficulty finding the right words. "I was disappointed when you turned me down."

Her heart lurched. Was this the moment she had been waiting for? Her skin tingled in nervous anticipation of what he would say next.

"Call it male arrogance or pride, but I didn't think you would refuse me."

She looked up into his eyes, seeking the truth. Was he in earnest or simply nursing a bruised ego? But she loved him with all her heart, so did it matter? "I didn't intend to injure your pride. Consider yourself fortunate. I haven't a penny to my name."

"What does money have to do with this?"

"Edwin, I'm not so naive as to believe all marriages are made in Heaven. My aunt is determined to find me a rich husband, but I'm not Cecilly. I won't miss the life she's been accustomed to. I'd rather make my own way. I'd prefer to be a governess again, than to sell myself to a wealthy man." She held her head high because she was speaking the truth, but in her heart she wanted nothing more than to love him.

"Would a rich husband offend your pride or is it marriage you're afraid of?" His last question struck a raw nerve. She didn't answer. "Marriage protects women; it's not to be feared."

Gently she felt his hand under her chin draw her mouth towards his. *Is he going to kiss me?*

"I want to protect you, Lucy."

"I know, but how do you feel about me?"

"I admire and respect you."

His answer disappointed her. There was no mention of affection. "And love, Edwin? Do you love me?" She had asked the question, and now she waited nervously for his answer.

"Of course, I care for you."

His answer wasn't enough for her, and her heart ached with disappointment. He admired and respected her, he cared for her, but he didn't love her. The realisation ran through her veins like a polar storm, freezing the warmth and passion that she felt for him. What would it take to melt her heart? One kiss, three little words, and she would be his forever.

Chapter Nine

Lucy wrote in her journal:

Sunday April 14th

We have been at sea for three days. The mornings are bright, but I am missing my newspapers. Daily bulletins via the Marconi Service are posted, but only in the first-class smoking room! Ladies are not allowed, so I have to pester Edwin and Marshall. I daren't ask Uncle Leyster for the daily snippets. The gentlemen must think I'm an egghead. Time passes quickly with dinner parties, dancing, and concerts. Everywhere I hear words of admiration for the ship. I agree. She is all the designers and builders claimed—comfortable, secure, and safe.

Cecily has recovered from her malady. She attributes the restoration of her health to Dr. O'Loughlin's medicine. She now joins us for meals, however, she eats very little. We are meeting Edwin and Marshall, shortly, who have promised to escort us up to the Boat Deck to watch the captain's inspection.

Lucy laid down her pen. She wanted to write about the fear which dried her mouth every time she saw a man who resembled the Comte D'Every. But she daren't commit the words to paper. And Edwin? If only he loved her, as she loved him. Not writing down her innermost thoughts protected them and kept them safe from prying eyes. It would never do if her journal fell into Aunt Maud's hands.

There was a knock at the door. "It's Lieutenant-Commander Hardie and Mr. Johnson," Monique said.

"Are you ready Lucy?" Cecilly asked.

Lucy tucked her journal under her pillow and followed her cousin into the corridor. Cecilly took Hardie's arm, leaving Marshall to escort Lucy.

"It's getting colder," Marshall shuddered as they emerged on the Boat Deck, "but invigorating."

"Like flying?" Lucy turned her face out of the wind.

Marshall leaned closer to her. "The sea is a challenging mistress, but nothing compares with crossing the ocean by soaring through the air."

Lucy gazed up to the sky, broken only by a solitary puff of white cloud. Then she saw a bird, hovering on the wind, its wings outstretched, and she understood perfectly. "Look, there's a bird following the ship. It must be wonderful to fly."

"There's nothing like it. I'll get another machine when I've settled some business in Washington." Marshall pressed himself closer to her. "I'd like to take you flying."

Lucy gripped the ship's rail. She had tried to heed Edwin's warning and distance herself from Marshall. Evidently, from his behaviour today, she had not been successful. He appeared to take every opportunity to be near to her, sometimes to the exclusion of the others. The idea of flying intrigued her, but she couldn't possibly accept his invitation.

"Lucy!" Cecilly called, hurrying towards her. "Hardie's been explaining the Marconi system to me. Did you know it's all sent in code?"

Lucy smiled. "Yes, isn't it fascinating that our messages can be sent through the air?"

"I'm going to ask Papa if I can send a Marconigram to Frank."

Looking over her cousin's shoulder, Lucy caught Edwin's dark eyes. "I'm sure he will be delighted to receive your greeting, but you will have to keep it short."

* * * *

Lucy and the Grants were joined at Sunday Service by Edwin and Marshall. It was held in the first-class dining room and was led by Captain Smith. He looked commanding standing before them, gold rings gleaming from the sleeves of his frock-coat uniform.

"We shall now sing Hymn number 418," Captain Smith announced. As Lucy flicked to the relevant page, she stole a sideways glance at Edwin standing beside her. Soon they would be in America, their days filled with social rounds as Cecilly made her mark on New York society. If Mr. Johnson Senior wasn't too ill, perhaps there might be a summer wedding.

But what of Edwin? New York meant a decision for her, too. She loved him. Whenever she saw him, she felt the same stomach clenching moment she had experienced the first morning they had met in London. But would theirs be a loveless marriage, at least on his part?

He wanted her, she knew it—hadn't she felt the passion and urgency of his kisses? But was that only the lust Cecilly had described?

Her mind flashed back to the previous night when Monique had left, and she had climbed into bed.

Cecilly had popped her head up over the silk covered eiderdown. "Marshall's in love."

"Really?" Lucy had feigned disinterest.

"Believe me I know about these things. Those sketches and pastels he keeps doing of you give him away completely."

"He's done several of you."

"Yes, and have you seen them? He takes twice as long over you. And yours come out looking beautiful."

"Nonsense, his drawings of you are just as good, if not better."

"Humbug! He's only got eyes for you. But there's nothing as romantic as an artistic spirit in love. As soon as he lands in New York, he'll make you an offer. I know it. And I'm sure your father will make no objection, especially when he knows my parents approve. Don't you see? We could both be married and in New York Society together."

"Don't get carried away with fanciful ideas. I wouldn't marry Marshall if he begged me."

"Heavens, how could you turn him down? Are you mad? Catches like him come once in a lifetime for girls like you—" Cecilly's hand had flown to her mouth. "I didn't mean it."

"Why not? It's the truth. I'm not embarrassed to be a poor relation. I've never been anything else. Listen, Cecilly, marry Frank. You love him, and there's no better reason for marriage. But don't push me into a loveless match. I like Marshall. He has become a friend, just a friend."

"But you don't love him."

"Precisely."

"What are you going to do? We shall have to find you someone. Oh, if only Hardie had money, but Mama says the Devincourts always marry money. She says I was wrong to encourage you in his direction."

Cecilly's words had cut deep. Edwin had proposed, once, and Uncle Leyster had promised a dowry. She didn't expect it to be large, hardly anything in comparison to Cecilly's, but there was something she wanted that money could not buy. If only Edwin could fall in love with her.

The sound of the congregation rising to leave jolted Lucy back to the present.

* * * *

As it was too chilly to sit out on the Boat Deck, Cecilly and Lucy, escorted by Edwin, found a table near a bay window in the reception lounge. Marshall joined them shortly afterwards. He sat down next to Cecilly but kept looking at his pocket watch.

"What's wrong?" she asked.

"At noon they post the ship's run. I'm in the sweepstake."

"What's that?"

Marshall pocketed his watch. "Each day gentlemen gamble on the distance the ship has steamed since the previous day. What do you reckon, Hardie? As a Navy man you must have a fair idea."

Lucy sensed the rivalry rising between the two men. She glanced at Edwin. Usually, he refused to be drawn, and she admired him for it.

"We've been building our speed steadily," he replied. "Currently I'd say we're making about twenty knots, perhaps more. The second day's run was five hundred and nineteen, so I'd go for five hundred and forty nautical miles or thereabouts."

"I'm on at five hundred fifty-five," Marshall declared, "but rumour has it the engines are turning three revolutions faster than normal running."

Edwin raised his eyebrows. "Generally rumours are started to mislead the gullible."

Marshall opened his mouth to reply but was drowned out by the siren sounding noon. He leapt to his feet. "If you'll excuse me, ladies, Hardie?" Without waiting for a reply, he hurried aft.

"Hardie," Cecilly said, "did Lucy mention I sent my maid to the Purser's office with a Marconigram for Frank? After you told me about the service yesterday, I asked Papa. He agreed but said I could only send one per day. It's so exciting sending messages across the ocean. I can't wait for Frank to reply. I do hope his father isn't seriously ill."

"I'm sure he will be pleased to receive it," Hardie said.

"I told him about the anniversary party tonight and how I would miss him. Imagine, Lucy, my parents have been married twenty years!"

The way Cecilly spoke made Lucy smile. "You make twenty years sound like a life sentence."

"I'm sure it is to some people, but it won't be to Frank and me." Cecilly twisted her diamond engagement ring around on her finger as she spoke.

"Don't look now, Cecilly, but Colonel Astor and his wife have just entered the lounge." Lucy said.

"We must get an introduction. Imagine, Madeleine Astor can have anything she wants."

"But is she happy?"

Cecilly shrugged, and Marshall returned with a long face.

"How many miles have we steamed?" Lucy asked, although she suspected he hadn't won.

"Five-forty-six." He sat down in the same leather chair he had vacated a few minutes before.

"Will we get to New York earlier than expected?" Cecilly asked.

Edwin leaned towards her. "Unlikely, Miss Grant. At this time of year, the waters we are currently sailing through are known for their ice packs. Captain Smith is bound to hold back for fear of damage."

"Damage? Did you say damage, Hardie? What possible damage could be done to a ship like this?" Cecilly asked.

"Ice breaks off the melting glaciers in Greenland and drifts slowly southwards. A captain posts extra lookouts when he enters an ice field. If icebergs are sighted, they're usually large, so it's possible to steer around them, thus avoiding a collision."

"Collision? I don't understand," Cecily said.

"Icebergs can be several hundred feet high and they float. They are dangerous because only about a tenth protrudes above the surface of the ocean. The danger is in what's concealed beneath," Hardie explained.

"It's been known for a 'berg to rip open the hull of a ship," Marshall said, "and if a ship's holed below her waterline, she'll let in the water."

Cecily gasped. "My goodness, but not to this ship—she's unsinkable. Frank said so."

Marshall chuckled. "There's nothing to worry about, Miss Grant. The *Titanic's* got a double-bottomed hull and eight water-tight doors. Even if she were holed, which is most unlikely, she'll still float. Why, I doubt if one of the new torpedoes could sink us."

Lucy patted her cousin's hand. "There, you see Cecily, there's nothing to worry about. The warships, don't they have heavy plating and double-bottomed hulls for protection?"

Marshall looked slightly stunned. "I suppose they do. But tell me, how does a young lady of quality know the secrets of the Admiralty?"

Lucy's jaw dropped open, but before she could speak Edwin said, "Miss Mainwaring reads the newspapers."

* * * *

After dinner that evening, the party moved to the lounge where coffee was served. A large group of people had gathered to listen to the ship's orchestra. The concert finished with a selection from Offenbach. With the memory of the enchanting music lingering in her ears, Lucy accompanied Cecilly and Lady Grant to their staterooms.

Lucy tapped on the door and Monique let them in. It didn't take the maid long to help Cecilly out of her evening dress and underwear. Lucy had begun to undress herself, but she couldn't get out of her corset without Monique's help. Both girls were in bed when Monique left.

"Did you enjoy your parents' anniversary party?" Lucy asked.

"Oh, yes, but I do wish Frank was here. I know we have male company, but it isn't the same as having my dear Frank at my side. Time is dragging. I shall be very glad when we arrive in New York. I know gentlemen like to talk about engines, flying machines, and ships, but I find those topics boring."

Lucy listened patiently to the numerous compliments poured upon Frank as Cecilly persisted in talking about him. She was very grateful when Cecilly drifted off to sleep. Unfortunately, sleep eluded her.

Her thoughts were about Edwin. She hoped one day, in the not too distant future, he would come to love her as she loved him. Silently she prayed her wishes would not be in vain.

* * * *

Lucy sat bolt upright in bed. She thought she heard several deep thuds coming from the bowels of the ship. Then a din started, like a distant fog horn sounding continuously instead of in blasts. Why was the ship making so much noise in the middle of the night? She glanced across at Cecilly. As Lucy slipped out of bed, she could just make out her cousin's sleeping form in the darkness.

Her senses alert, she struggled to open the window and felt a cold draught rush in. However, it smelled odd. She closed her eyes and inhaled deeply. Where had she breathed similar air before? The ice cave on the Eiger, last year. Ice...it was ice!

Cecilly stirred, so she shut the window. Anxious to know what had happened, she fumbled for her drawers and slipped them on under her long, cotton nightgown. A pair of stockings, garters, and her navy woollen dress with the new Irish lace collar followed. Marshall hadn't mentioned the gift, so she had kept silent about it.

In the darkness she fumbled to fasten the front of her gown. Quickly she pushed her feet into her boots and tied the laces. It was dark in the stateroom, but if she switched on the electric light, it might waken Cecilly; then she wouldn't be able to go anywhere. Grabbing her coat, beret, and scarf, she closed the door quietly behind her and advanced a few steps along the corridor towards the stairway.

At the Grants' door she hesitated. She ought to inform them of her suspicions. She raised her clenched fist to knock but stopped. What time was it? Immediately she regretted not bringing her fob watch. Leaving them to their slumbers, she made for the stairway and ascended rapidly.

On the Boat Deck, the cold numbed her face. Only one gentleman stood there. On first sight of his solitary male figure, she halted. The comte? No, this man had an athletic appearance. He could have been a military man from his stance. She watched him for a few moments as he searched the blackness of the ocean.

He turned and seeing her, approached with his hands cupped around his mouth. He shouted over the din of escaping steam. "Can your young eyes see what's struck us, ma'am?"

Despite the loud roar of steam, Lucy picked up his deep, Southern drawl. "I can't see anything," she answered. "Have we been hit, sir?"

"Yes, ma'am, I reckon we have." He turned away from her and hurried along the deck. He stopped every few paces to claim any vantage point where his view wasn't blocked by the lifeboats.

Lucy hurried after him. The answer had to be ice, but she couldn't see any. She had begun to doubt her sense of smell, when the American gentleman turned to face her.

"Go below, ma'am," he bellowed. "Find your family and look after them!"

It came like an order, given with authority from one who had known command. She halted and watched him vault the iron gate which divided the first and second class areas of the Boat Deck. He moved towards the stern. She considered pursuing him, but doubted if she could manage the gate so easily. His orders had been specific, and she had no business being out alone at night. A pang of guilt gripped her, followed by fear. She had broken her promise to Edwin.

Descending the stairs, she turned to port and peered through the glass enclosing the whole of the Promenade Deck. The sky twinkled brightly with stars. The ocean glistened like jet. On her way back to her stateroom, she felt disappointed her venture had been in vain. Why discharge steam? Surely that meant loss of power.

Several people wandered along the corridor. She pulled her scarf around her face, not wishing to be recognised, especially when she passed Mr. Ismay, the President of White Star Line. Preoccupied with one of the ship's officers, he failed to acknowledge her. She was glad, although they had been introduced the previous day. His expression, like the American gentleman she had encountered on the Boat Deck, looked grave.

Back on B Deck, Mr. Ismay's haunting look remained with her. She blinked to rid herself of it but remembered her father's face the night her mother died. Her throat tightened. She tasted danger.

Cecilly was still asleep, when Lucy came back to the stateroom. Something was wrong. The American gentleman thought the ship had been hit—if so, this would be no ordinary night. She was about to wake Cecilly, when there was a firm knock on the door. She switched on the electric light. The knock came again, this time more urgently. Hesitantly, she opened the door a few inches.

"Awaken Cecilly and get dressed in your warmest clothes." Sir Leyster ordered. He still wore his evening dress and seemed not to notice Lucy's coat. "The stewardess will be along presently to help you into your life-preservers."

"Life-preservers!" She opened the door wider. "What's happened? Is the ship sinking?"

"The unsinkable *Titanic?*" His moustache twitched slightly. "Of course not, merely a precaution."

Lucy sensed the truth and stared back at him. She was about to say no ship was unsinkable when he turned away. Then he stopped and looked back at her.

"It would be most unwise to spread rumours, especially in front of Cecilly and her mother."

"Do you wish Cecilly and I to remain here?"

He dragged his hand through his hair as he nodded. "I'll bring your aunt here in a few minutes."

As she closed the door, an overwhelming feeling of foreboding washed over her. But there was no time to dwell upon it. "Wake up!" She shook her cousin. "You must get dressed at once! Get up, Cecilly!"

After another tap on the door, Lucy opened it to Monique. Immediately the maid took charge of waking and dressing her mistress.

"I'll wait outside; perhaps I can find out what's going on," Lucy said. Outside in the corridor she stopped a steward, "What's happening?"

"There nothing to worry about, Miss, just a bit of engine trouble. It'll soon be fixed."

Lucy didn't believe him, but her hopes were raised when an officer approached. Another lady waylaid him before he reached her. She moved closer, determined to eavesdrop on his answer to the question on everyone's lips. *Was there any danger?*

"None as far as I know, ma'am." The officer raised his hand to his cap. He strode past Lucy towards the staircase. Instinctively she followed him up to the Promenade Deck. When she saw him knock on the door of stateroom A36, she stepped closer. Mr. Andrews opened the door, his face solemn. The officer went inside.

Swiftly Lucy stationed herself at Mr. Andrews' door. It hadn't been closed properly. Gently she pressed against it, easing the solid wooden door open a few inches. She knew what she was doing was wrong, but her need for the truth prevailed.

"The captain's compliments, sir, he wishes to see you immediately. Will you accompany me to the bridge?"

"I'll need my charts to make accurate calculations," Mr. Andrews replied.

"All the water-tight doors have been secured, sir."

"Damage report?"

"We sighted an iceberg, went hard to starboard, and reversed all engines. She couldn't turn fast enough; we hit. The mail room is already flooding, sir."

Her suspicions confirmed, Lucy remained frozen to the spot. With her back to the door, she was blocking the entrance when the door opened fully.

"Excuse us." Mr. Andrews acknowledged her with a nod.

As she stepped out of the way, she addressed him directly. "There's no unsinkable ship, is there Mr. Andrews?"

Her words appeared to stun him momentarily. His chin dropped and he closed his eyes. Lucy thought he wasn't going to answer her impertinence. When he raised his head, his expression was gaunt. "No, Miss Mainwaring, there isn't."

She stepped aside. "Oh, God help us." She covered her face with her hands and prayed for inner strength. When she looked up the two men had left. Nervously, she hurried back towards her stateroom, down the stairs and along corridor, now filling with people.

Edwin was waiting for her outside the stateroom. "Where have you been?"

She threw her arms around his neck. "The ship's sinking!"

He unwrapped her arms and held her firmly by the shoulders. "She's hit an iceberg, but she's not done for yet."

"I've just seen Mr. Andrews and he—"

"Hush, Sir Leyster's coming," Edwin released his hold on her.

Lucy glanced at her uncle, he looked worried. "You must not go wandering off, Lucy, do you understand? We must stay together."

"Yes," she nodded, realising she had added to her uncle's concern by trying to satisfy her own curiosity.

"May I have a private word with Lucy?" Hardie asked.

Sir Leyster looked at them both in turn. He took out his pocket watch and flicked open the case. "You can have five minutes, no more."

Edwin took her elbow and guided her along the corridor to his stateroom. Inside, Lucy paced nervously. "I know the ship is sinking. I saw Mr. Andrews. I saw his face. He designed her. He knows about the damage."

"Did *he* tell you the *Titanic* was sinking?"

She shook her head. "He didn't have to. I saw it in his face. And they won't tell us the worst, will they?"

He didn't answer.

"There must be over two thousand people on board, including the crew. Oh! Edwin, we've often strolled on the Boat Deck and—" she broke off, as the stark realisation of the dreadful truth hit her. "There aren't enough lifeboats."

He threw is head back and glared at the ceiling. "There's no question of people being put into lifeboats."

She threw her arms around him and linked them behind his neck. "Tell me the truth, Edwin, please. I counted sixteen boats the other day. If they can hold a hundred each, that's still not enough, is it?"

His jaw muscles twitched. He lowered his chin and looked directly into her eyes. Gently he cupped her face in his hands. "I can't hide much from you, dearest, can I?" He lifted her face towards his and their lips met.

She felt the warmth of his body only inches from hers as he kissed her with the same passion he'd used to claim her in the conservatory. But now his kisses became more demanding, willing her to surrender to him. His hands slipped around her, drawing her ever closer.

Her heart pounded as she responded to his caresses. Every inch of her awakened and lifeblood surged through her veins. Her fingers caressed the nape of his neck. She almost forgot any fears she harboured as sensations, previously unknown, flooded through her body.

"I want you so much," he confessed, depositing light kisses along her jaw line.

Her throat dried. She closed her eyes. Was this the moment she had yearned for? Was he about to declare a love to match hers?

"I'm in earnest, Lucy, truly I am. I want you. I want you to be mine. Marry me, Lucy. Please be my wife."

Was this the time to say yes, to fulfill her needs and his? Was she ready to confess her love and to hear him say those precious words? She opened her eyes and hoped to see love's joy in his. There was only blackness, like the ocean surrounding them. Something was wrong.

Urgently she searched his face. What had brought him to the point of desperation?

"We're sinking, aren't we?" She felt his answer through his touch. "Hold me close, please."

He dropped several soft kisses on her cheek. "There is some danger. You must be very brave and go with the rest of the women and children. I'm being selfish, I know, pressing you like this. I have no right, but I do want to marry you."

"Edwin, I—"

"Can't you say yes?" He squeezed her body firmly. "Time is short, and we must get back to the others."

"Time?" She fell silent, inwardly gathering her strength. "The *Titanic* is sinking, isn't she?"

"Yes," he hissed through clenched teeth. He let out an exasperated sigh and took her hands in his. "I know this isn't the right time, or the right place, but please say you'll be mine."

Lucy's agile mind raced. Had he been driven by their plight to cast all care to the wind and propose? He said he needed her, wanted her, but he hadn't said he loved her. But if he did act rashly, would it be wrong to grant his wish? It was hers too, but was his that of a man facing death? She shut her eyes and searched for inner strength. She wanted desperately to ask him if he loved her. But would she be asking an honest man to lie?

She closed her mind to doubt. "I will marry you, Edwin, and if you change your mind in New York, I'll jolly well sue you for breach of promise."

No sooner had she uttered her futile threat then he lifted her up off her feet and swung her around. They were interrupted by a sharp knock on the door. The steward entered with a life-preserver under his arm.

"Give it to Miss Mainwaring." Edwin pulled on an overcoat over his evening suit. "I must present myself to Captain Smith and offer him my assistance."

The thick, cork-filled garment felt bulky, but not heavy. Once Lucy had it on, the steward showed her how to buckle it correctly. "I suggest you put on warm clothing, Miss Mainwaring, and make your way to the lifeboats. Is there anything else, sir?"

Edwin shook his head. "Go, others need help."

The steward made for the door. "Good luck, sir, Miss Mainwaring."

When he had gone, Lucy reached up to Edwin and turned his face towards hers. Fear clasped its heavy hand around her heart. "What is the captain doing?"

"He'll order the Marconi men to call any ships in the vicinity. He'll fill the lifeboats with women and children and pray the engineers can keep her afloat until help arrives. Once the ladies are off safely, Sir Leyster and I will take our chances with the rest of the men and crew. There's probably a ship steaming for us now. Thanks to the Marconi Service, half the North Atlantic will know we're in trouble. I'll take you back to Sir Leyster." He leaned closer. "Best to keep quiet about the ship, especially in front of Cecilly. She's unpredictable."

Lucy nodded and turned towards the door. She felt clumsy in the life-preserver and yearned for the strength of Edwin's arms around her again.

"Take this, please." He offered her his gold pocket watch.

"I can't."

"Nonsense, it was my grandfather's." He flicked open the case. "It's sixteen minutes past midnight. By my reckoning we were hit at fourteen minutes to. Look after it for me, will you?" He didn't wait for an answer. He closed the case with a click and forced the watch into her hand.

People rushed past the open door. The steward hovered close by, waiting to lock the empty stateroom behind them. Coiling the heavy chain into the palm of her hand, Lucy pushed Edwin's watch down the front of her gown, next to her heart. Hand in hand they abandoned the stateroom together.

Chapter Ten

Horrified, Lucy could not believe the chaos that reigned when she returned to her stateroom. Cecilly's entire wardrobe appeared to be piled on top of the beds as she sorted through her many gowns with Monique's assistance. Lady Grant, her portly figure swelled by her life-preserver, sat clutching her jewel case. She was attended by her personal maid, Miss Jenkins.

"Cecilly, whatever are you doing?" Lucy cried. "You are supposed to get dressed, not pack everything!"

"I'm not going anywhere without my Paris gowns."

"Leave the luggage, we must go to the Promenade Deck and stand ready for the lifeboats. You must wear warm clothing and put on your life-preserver. There's no time to lose."

Cecilly ignored her. She continued to pick up gowns and discard them as if choosing one for a garden party. Lucy turned around and bumped into her uncle. How long he had been standing there, she didn't know.

"Ladies!" He bellowed. For a few seconds silence prevailed.

"We should never have boarded this ship." Lady Grant said.

"Shut up, Maud."

"What's wrong, Papa?"

"Cecilly, why aren't you dressed?" He gave Monique a sharp look. "Attend to your mistress. Warm clothes, no luggage, and wear the life-preservers. All of you."

"Yes, sir, at once," the maid replied.

"I want everyone ready to leave when I return. You have five minutes, ladies, no more!" He turned and left.

As she was already dressed, Lucy picked up a coat for Cecilly. Then remembering how cold it was outside, she gathered scarves, gloves, and two steamer rugs. She pushed the spare gloves into her pockets. Both maids hurried to get Cecilly dressed as ordered.

When Sir Leyster returned he led them up to the Promenade Deck, but it was already crowded when they arrived. The loud roar of escaping steam ceased, and an uncanny silence befell the throng. Gradually the buzz of conversation recommenced. "It is too crowded here; follow me to the lounge." Sir Leyster said.

Once inside Lucy saw Marshall squeezing between groups of passengers as he made his way towards them. "Good evening," he said.

She gave him a friendly smile and immediately regretted encouraging him. She was engaged! But who knew it? Did it matter? She and Edwin had the rest of their lives. She shivered. *Didn't they?*

"Let me carry those for you, Miss Mainwaring." Marshall pointed to the steamer rugs she had brought from the stateroom.

She watched him tuck his brown leather satchel behind his back between his life-preserver and his overcoat.

"Sketches of you, my portfolio's most valuable possession," he whispered in her ear.

His mouth widened into a satisfied grin, and she blushed. He stood so close she felt his hot breath on her cheek. For a split second panic seized her. He was teasing her, she convinced herself. How crass of him to trifle with her when they were facing imminent danger. But did he know how serious their situation was? Perhaps not, so she dismissed his impertinence with a cold stare and gave him the rugs.

Her dismissive glare wasn't enough. A few moments later, when she looked back at him, his cavalier smile was displayed for anyone to see. "Mr. Marshall, this is hardly the time or place for frivolity."

"Believe me, Lucy, nothing is more important to me at this precise moment than you."

"Mr. Marshall, please, I do not want to hear any more."

"But this is the first chance I've had to speak to you alone for days," he said.

"Mr. Marshall, stop this foolishness." She looked around, anywhere to avoid eye contact with him. There were more people in the first-class lounge than she had ever seen in there before. Standing by one of the long windows, she could see onto the Promenade Deck which was less crowded than before. People hurried by, but she could see no sign of boats being loaded. *Are we waiting in the right place?* But there were no officers or crew to ask.

Lucy noticed how people collected together in groups. Some stood around, worry and fear etched on their faces. In contrast, others laughed and joked. Dress varied enormously too. She jostled with people, like herself, wearing the bulky life-preservers, whilst others slipped by as if dressed for dinner. Perhaps the gentlemen in evening suits didn't fully understand their predicament. Then swallowing deeply, she looked again; perhaps they understood their situation perfectly.

Time slipped by, and the atmosphere grew tense. Faces grimaced as anxiety gave way to impatience and frustration followed. There were no officers to reassure the passengers or tell them where to go. Lucy became aware of her foot tapping the carpet and forced herself to stay still. Closing her eyes, she hoped a few moments inner reflection might restore her fading confidence. She gripped her hands together and prayed for a miracle. *Let another ship pass by. Let someone hear our distress call!* Whilst she placed her faith in God, silently she thanked Mr. Marconi.

Sir Leyster reached under his life-preserver for his pocket watch. He glanced at the time and snapped the case shut. "Where are the ship's officers?"

At that moment the small orchestra struck up a cheerful ragtime tune. The music, perhaps representing a return to normality, quieted the hum of conversation. Lucy noticed the change. Lifted by the music, people looked less tense. She stretched on tip-toe and glanced around her. *How can they be so unaffected by the danger?* Her heart pounded, yet was she guilty of funnelling her own anxiety into the faces of others? *They refuse to believe this ship is sinking because as long as they cling to the notion of infallibility, there is sense and order in their world.*

She gnawed nervously on her clenched fist. The bitter taste and pungent smell of kid leather caused a wave of nausea to sweep up from her stomach. She swallowed the bile and said a quick prayer.

"Oh, you beautiful doll, you great big beautiful doll." Marshall sang along with the band.

"How can you sing at a time like this?" Lucy glared at him.

"Why not? I often sing when I'm flying—helps pass the time. Excellent for the lungs, unless the engine's spluttering oil, then it might be dangerous. I do wish something would happen. All this waiting around makes me feel like a fish out of water."

Lucy thought his joke in bad taste, but realised he must be feeling the strain too.

"I'd rather fly over the ocean than sail. In the air I'm in control. Down here, waiting with all these other folks, I feel like a trussed up turkey waiting to be roasted for Thanksgiving."

"It's absolutely intolerable," Cecilly said. "How dare they drag us from our warm beds in the middle of the night? Why do we have to stand around here for hours? I'm tired of waiting.

Mother was right. If I'd known it was going to be like this, I'd never have agreed to come."

"You would have disappointed Frank." Lucy hoped by mentioning his name it would draw her cousin out of her moodiness.

"Frank! When will I see him?" Her gloved hand flew to her lips. "He's to meet us at the dock on Wednesday morning. Goodness knows what time we shall reach New York now."

"We'll be surrounded by rescue ships in no time," Marshall said. "Most likely they'll tow this sea goddess the rest of the way. So there's no need to worry. You'll see Frank in a few days for sure."

Cecilly clasped her hands together then began rubbing her fingers. She stopped and pulled the glove from her left hand. "My ring! I've lost Frank's ring!"

Several people turned around at the shrill sound of her voice. Lucy grabbed her wrist. "Did you put it on?"

"I don't know, I keep it in a special box. Next to my bed." She looked up at her father. "What am I going to do?"

He eyed her sternly. "Pull yourself together."

She burst into tears and sought her mother's embrace.

Lucy wanted to help; she turned to her uncle. "They haven't started loading the boats yet. I'll go back to the stateroom and get it."

"Nonsense," Sir Leyster snapped. "You're not going anywhere alone."

Marshall stepped forward. "Sir, it would be a privilege to escort Miss Mainwaring."

Sir Leyster frowned and drew Lucy to one side. "I don't trust him."

"I know," Lucy whispered. "Edwin told me, but it's only a short distance, and Cecilly is very distressed. I'm sure Mr. Marshall won't let any harm befall me."

"Very well," Sir Leyster nodded. "Take care, my dear. If either Edwin or my valet return, I'll send them to meet you."

"Monique, take these rugs from Mr. Marshall. We'll need them in the lifeboat. I won't be long," Lucy said.

＊ ＊ ＊ ＊

"It's locked!" Lucy cried, rattling the door handle.

"Company procedure," Marshall snorted. "White Star can't have any of its first-class passengers robbed."

"Your sarcasm is ill-timed. Is the stewardess around?"

He strode towards an open stateroom and called to the stewardess. She emerged, keys in hand. "I can let you in, Miss, but I can't stay. I have to help another lady into her life-preserver." Quickly she unlocked the door.

Marshall, who had waited in the corridor, stuck his head around the open door. "I've just seen Mr. Andrews. I'll catch up with him. He'll know what's up for sure. When you've found the ring, stay here. I'll come back for you."

Flooding the room with light, Lucy struggled over the piles of clothes and found the ring in its box beside Cecilly's bed. She pushed the box into her pocket and turned to leave. Marshall stood in the doorway, white-faced, his amicable mask finally stripped away.

"Are you all right?" She assumed he had not only caught up with Andrews but had also learned the ship's fate. "What did he say?"

"Nothing to worry about." He shrugged as he entered the room.

"I don't believe you. It's bad, isn't it? The *Titanic's* done for."

He moved towards her, his eyes half-crazed. "How did you know?"

"I saw their faces: the officers, Mr. Andrews, Mr. Ismay, and my uncle. They were filled with hopelessness and disbelief."

"So that's why you looked at me so strangely just now? What chance has a fellow got with you, Lucy? Why a chap can't even lie his way out of corner to save his life." He flicked his hair out of his eyes. "Looks like Fate's dealt few winning hands tonight."

"I've got the ring. We must get back." She stepped towards him, but he blocked her path.

"I've never admired a woman more than you. And I didn't really know it myself, until now."

"We must go back, I insist." She didn't want to hear anymore. She moved towards the door, but he barred her way.

"I can't let you go. I'd do anything for you, Lucy."

"No. You don't understand—"

"On the contrary, Miss Mainwaring," a third voice interjected. "I'm beginning to understand perfectly."

Lucy let out a gasp of horror when she recognised the Comte D'Every behind his beard and gold-rimmed spectacles.

"Inside." He prodded Marshall and forced him into the stateroom. Without turning around he kicked the door shut behind him. "Get back!"

Lucy bit hard on her bottom lip as she stared at the revolver pointed at her. She felt Marshall place his arm around her.

"You know what I've come for," the comte said.

"I haven't the slightest idea," Marshall replied.

The comte chuckled. "Miss Mainwaring, I had no idea you were in league with Marshall. I thought your patriotic allegiance lay elsewhere. A great pity we could not have come to an arrangement. In our business, a woman like you is a rare commodity."

Lucy froze. The meeting she had been dreading had finally come. Fear, as cold as ice, crept down her vertebrae. Around the headband of her beret, beads of sweat gathered, and her mouth dried. He terrified her, but she couldn't look away, as if holding his attention meant staying alive.

"Sadly, I have no time to dwell on what might have been. I want those plans, Marshall." "The plans or your lives—which is it to be?" His mouth twisted into a sadistic smile.

Lucy froze. What did he mean? She had no plans.

The comte pointed the gun at her. "Miss Mainwaring, move away from Marshall."

Slowly, her legs heavy, Lucy eased herself across the room, picking her way through the piles of gowns and accessories Cecilly had scattered around.

Marshall moved forward. "Plans? What plans? You're scrounging around after pieces of paper? I thought you'd be with the rest of the rats, first to abandon a sinking ship."

The comte fired a shot above Marshall's head. Lucy screamed.

"That's a warning. The next one's for her." The comte pulled off his wire-rimmed glasses and threw them aside. His eyes narrowed to slits as he stepped towards Lucy, but he caught his foot in the strap of an open case and stumbled. Marshall leapt upon him, and the two men struggled.

As the men grappled for control of the weapon, Lucy drew back in horror. Another shot went off. Instinctively she covered her ears, as the men fought on without regard for her or each other. Marshall knocked the gun out of the comte's hands, and it disappeared amongst the debris of Cecilly's wardrobe.

"Do something!" Marshall cried out, as the comte seized him by the throat.

Edging her way to the dressing table, Lucy grabbed a heavy crystal vase and struck the comte on the back of his head. He slumped to the floor.

"Thanks, that was becoming a close run thing!" Marshall said.

"God forgive me!" she cried, taking deep breaths. "What have I done?"

He took her in his arms. "Hush, you've knocked him out, that's all. He'll have a mighty sore head when he comes round in a few minutes." He guided her to the edge of the bed and sat her down. Bending on one knee, he checked on the comte.

"He's not dead?"

"Of course not. I'll put him over here." He dragged the unconscious comte to the other side of the bed where he couldn't be seen from the doorway.

There was a brief knock on the open door, and the stewardess entered. "Forgive the intrusion, but I heard loud bangs. You must go on deck. The boats are loading, Miss, and I can't be responsible any longer. Please, Miss. I have to lock the door. You must hurry."

"I'll see Miss Mainwaring to the boats. Quickly, this way." He grabbed Lucy's arm and rushed her along the corridor. He halted at the end, next to the exit to the stairway and pulled her towards him. He took her chin lightly between his forefinger and thumb and dropped a soft kiss on her lips.

She tried to push him away. His kiss, although warm and loving, left her cold. There could only be one man for her. She freed herself from Marshall's embrace and turned towards the open staircase. Edwin was standing there.

He stared at her for a few agonising moments. "Sir Leyster is worried about you. The lifeboats are loading. This way!"

Her heart filled with tension. She wanted to explain about Marshall, but was there time?

"Edwin!" She propelled herself forward. "It's not what you think. I didn't want Marshall to come with me."

He took her arm, and they scurried up the stairs. They covered the Promenade Deck at speed. Lucy gazed around; many of the women had gone, and she couldn't see Cecilly, Lady Grant, or their maids. Her heart pounded. With every ounce of energy she could muster she grasped Edwin's arm and threw herself in front of him. "I love you, Edwin, whatever you may think of me. Always remember I love you!"

"I know," he said, his face etched with pain.

"Where the Hell is Sir Leyster's party?" Marshall demanded as he caught up with them.

Edwin eyed him suspiciously. "Up on the Boat Deck. There are problems getting the last boats away. She's listing. Panic has broken out. It's women and children only."

"Lucy must get to a boat." Marshall yanked her elbow, and together the two men frog-marched her up to the Boat Deck.

The scene confronting her proved totally different from the happy hours she had spent walking with Edwin on the Boat Deck. Groups of men stood alone. The ship's davits hung ghostly empty now that the lifeboats had gone. Lucy looked aft to the poop deck, now crowded with passengers. Men shouted, women screamed, and somewhere in the background she heard music—ragtime, lively, and rollicking. Marshall pushed in front of them and leaned over the ship's rail, scanning the ocean.

Lucy felt very small. She looked up into Edwin's eyes, hoping to find compassion there. "I'm sorry, Edwin, truly I am."

"I know." He spoke mechanically without looking at her.

"Most of the boats are away," Marshall shouted, "but there's a boat swung out down on the Promenade Deck that's still not loaded. It's our best bet for Lucy."

A tremendous roar zoomed skywards as three pairs of eyes followed the path of a rocket launched from the starboard side of the ship. "God's teeth," Edwin swore.

The noise made Lucy jump. She clung to Edwin's arm. "What's that?"

"A rescue ship's close. We're letting them know we're here," Marshall said.

"Believe that if you like, Marshall, but those are distress rockets. We're lit from bow to stern and the ocean's calm. Captain Smith is signalling any small vessel laid to for the night."

Marshall turned to Lucy. "We must get you back to the Promenade Deck. Even if we can't find Sir Leyster, you're going in that lifeboat. Isn't she, Hardie?"

Lucy noticed Marshall's mouth narrow as he eyed his rival. Edwin replied with a curt nod. Again they marched her towards the Grand Staircase, passing the band, who continued to play. The list on the ship made it increasingly difficult to descend the wide stairs. Halfway down, they met Captain Smith coming up. He wore his great coat and hat, both heavily embossed with the gold braid of authority.

"Help will be needed to launch the collapsible." He said to Hardie in a calm voice.

"Captain," Lucy spoke up, "which ships are coming to our aid?" Before tonight she might have blushed at the directness of her question. With their situation reaching desperation, she demanded an answer.

He didn't hesitate with his reply. "The *Carpathia* is steaming full-speed to join us. She'll be here soon, but I'd like all the ladies in the lifeboats." He raised his hand to his cap and saluted her.

Neither Lucy nor her two escorts replied. The glazed look in the captain's eyes made Lucy think of the information he had neglected to impart. Would the *Titanic* still be afloat when the *Carpathia* arrived?

On the Promenade Deck a crowd of men surrounded an open window. Outside, the lifeboat hung parallel to the side. An officer was supervising the loading of the lifeboat. To Lucy's relief she spied the Grant party amongst the crowd.

Cecilly threw her arms around Lucy's neck. "We were so worried about you. Did you get the ring?"

Withdrawing the small ivory box from her pocket, Lucy pressed it into her cousin's hand. Cecily held it close to her chest for a few moments. "I'll never let it out of my sight again. Thank you so much, Lucy."

"Maud, you are going in that boat!" Sir Leyster shouted.

Lady Grant shook her head.

Gradually ladies started to board, several weeping. Some carried babies; others had older children with them, holding onto their skirts. Waiting in front of the Grant party Lucy recognised Colonel Astor and his wife, Madeleine.

The officer helped Mrs. Astor aboard followed by her nurse and a maid. A hushed silence fell over the waiting crowd. The colonel stepped forward to follow his wife.

"No, sir," the officer called. "No men allowed in these boats until all the women are loaded."

"Goodbye, I'll follow in another boat," Colonel Astor said to his wife. He turned to the officer. "What number is this boat?"

"Number Four, sir."

Cecily turned towards her father and gave him a generous hug, which he returned. He released her, and she boarded the lifeboat.

"You're next, Maud." Lady Grant shook her head. "Twenty years ago you promised to obey me—now get in that boat!" Sir Leyster stepped towards his wife, grabbed her arm, and pecked her cheek.

The colour had drained from her face, her expression like a death-mask. She showed no emotion as she turned towards the exit. Two crewmen hauled her through the open window. The Grants' maids, Monique and Miss Jenkins, followed their mistresses.

"My dear Lucy," Sir Leyster said softly. "I believe the time has come for me to stand aside." He nodded to Edwin.

She stretched up on tip-toe and boldly claimed Edwin's lips. His arms came up and he hugged her firmly. "I'll never forget my promise, Edwin," she whispered. "I love you, and tomorrow will always belong to us..." Her voice trailed off as tears welled up inside her. She stepped towards the open window but kept her eyes on him for as long as she could. He held her future happiness in his hands. To never see him again would break her heart.

One step from the open window, Marshall pushed his way forward and forced his satchel into her hand. "Take this, Lucy; it was my future. Do what you want with it. I bequeath it to you. Forgive me for loving you, Lucy, but I couldn't help myself."

As she opened her mouth to speak, he grabbed her and kissed her passionately. It was a brief, stolen kiss which shocked her and left her cold. She pulled away from him. Stunned, she searched for Edwin. Her eyes blurred hot with tears. She needed to see forgiveness in his face. He had to be the last person she saw on the sinking ship, as he would always be in her heart.

Chapter Eleven

The moment Lucy left the ship, the cold night air stung her face. Her lips trembled at the gallery of long-faced men looking down at the lifeboat. Crushed against the gunwale, she craned her neck, desperate to use every possible second to fix Edwin's image in her mind. She wanted to know that every time she blinked she would be able to see him at will. She had no photograph or likeness of him, except the picture imprinted on her memory. She remembered his gold watch, nestled between her breasts. She put her hand on her chest and pressed his watch and chain against her heart for safekeeping.

The lifeboat lurched. Women screamed. "We'll all be drowned!" An anguished cry echoed through the night air. Lucy understood their plight; it was hers too. Afraid the freezing water would engulf them, her heart pounded. The wooden boat smacked the surface of the sea with an alarming clout. Lucy grabbed the side to steady herself.

"The water's up to D Deck!" A voice screeched from the blackness. There followed a collective gasp. Lucy looked at the stunned faces surrounding her. Most were passengers, like her aunt, who had probably stood by whilst others left in earlier lifeboats. Perhaps they had been convinced of the ship's infallibility? But now, Lucy saw in their faces the stark reality of imminent disaster. Many, like her aunt, sat in shocked silence, squashed together in Boat Four, eyes riveted to the rising ocean.

"Cast off the blocks!" the officer from above bellowed. "Go to the stern hatch and pick up some men to crew."

Adjusting her eyes to the blackness in the lifeboat, Lucy managed to pick out the outline of two crewmen, one at the stern, the other at the bow. Each struggled to free the ropes. "We need another hand down here," one of them yelled.

Another crewman answered from above and slid down the rope still attached to the davit. He took charge, freed the blocks, and got the oars ready. "Give way together," he shouted. "Pull ladies! Row for your lives!"

"That's us," Lucy said to Cecilly. Together they tried to row, but they couldn't move the heavy oar. A loud crash vibrated through the wood. Cecilly winced and let go.

"Take hold, pull!" Lucy nudged her. No response. "Why can't you do this one thing to ease our plight?"

"I...can't!" Cecilly wailed.

"Try to concentrate." When Cecilly made no attempt to move the oar Lucy shouted, "Think of Frank...think of England! Pray to God...oh! I don't know. Just *row*."

"I can't."

"We must. When the ship goes down she'll pull us with her. We've got to get far enough away."

"The ship's not sinking..." Cecilly's girlish voice trailed off. "Papa!" she screeched, followed by a spine-chilling wail.

"Pull," Lucy demanded, "pull!"

It was no use. Cecilly clung to the oar, leaned her body over it, and wailed uncontrollably. Lucy could only partly shift it. The oar crashed into another and impeded their progress. "Miss Jenkins, look after Miss Grant. Monique, take her place and help me with this oar," Lucy said.

Eventually, working together, they dragged their oar laboriously in and out of the water. Somehow the seaman maneuvered the boat to the stern of the liner. The hatch was shut fast. He wasted no more time. He turned the rudder sharply and shouted for the oars to be pulled in unison. Slowly Boat Four pulled away from the stricken vessel.

Lucy glanced over her shoulder at the ship. The *Titanic* was brilliantly illuminated. Her electric lights burned defiantly from every window and porthole, as if she was determined to do down in blazing glory. Silhouetted figures hurried along her vast decks. Desperate people sought escape, any escape, as the sea swallowed the giantess deck by deck.

"Lord, please help them," Lucy prayed aloud.

"What did you say?" Cecilly lifted her head. She looked bewildered, as if she had just woken from a bad dream.

"Can you help with the rowing?" Lucy asked gently.

Cecilly stretched out her hands and grasped the oar. They hadn't gone far when she moaned. "I swear I'm getting blisters on my hands, like a common servant."

Lucy plunged her hand into her coat pocket and pulled out her spare pair of gloves. "Put these on." She pushed them towards her cousin. "Put them over yours, they'll help protect your hands."

Cecilly slipped them on. "I wish Mama would say something. I've never seen her like this before."

Lady Grant, who hadn't spoken since she had been parcelled aboard the lifeboat, sat straight-backed next to her daughter. Lucy gave her an anxious sideways glance, but it was too dark to see her face. Her aunt looked like a cardboard cutout, her stark profile motionless. Her head held high, she appeared very proud, but Lucy suspected she was in shock.

Lucy closed her eyes for a few seconds, and Edwin's image flashed before her. She winced as a pain stabbed her heart. "I must not give up hope," she mouthed softly to herself. She forced her eyes open and managed to give Cecilly an encouraging smile. Dearest Cecilly, she fluttered like a butterfly from one place, or activity, to another. She settled nowhere and created chaos in her wake, as she had done in their stateroom earlier. She had been told to dress, but could only think of her Paris gowns. And then she couldn't choose between them.

Lucy caught her breath...the stateroom. An image of the comte lying on the floor flashed before her. Had Marshall spoken the truth when he told her she had only knocked him out?

Anguished cries—male, deep and guttural—echoed across the dark waters.

"Over there!" a boy cried. His young voice was followed by a crescendo of desperate pleas for help.

"Hold to," ordered the seaman at the tiller. "There's men in the water nearby."

The ladies stopped rowing. Lucy scanned the ship. Fully lit, the *Titanic* lay ominously deep in the water.

"Look!" A young woman, sitting close to Lucy, yelled. "People are throwing wreckage into the sea."

Lucy bit down on her lip hard. The desperate situation facing those left onboard played out before her. Powerless to do anything to help, she scrutinised the Boat Deck, where hundreds of tiny figures swarmed towards the liner's stern like ants. She focused on a group of men. They were in danger of being washed into the sea at any moment. Together they fought to free a small, unturned boat stowed on the roof of the officers' quarters. The hull was white, but the dark ocean was about to engulf the tiny boat. Silently she prayed for the men's success. It was all she could do.

The *Titanic's* bow awash, Lucy watched as her stern rose out of the water. Above the constant screams came a tremendous crashing noise, as if thousands of pieces of bone china shattered simultaneously. Lucy shuddered. *Where are they now?* Her heart wept—Edwin, Sir Leyster, Marshall. Fearing for them, she struggled to keep hold of her emotions. *There will be time for tears tomorrow. I mustn't give up hope.*

Perhaps the *Titanic* could keep afloat until a rescue ship arrived? Captain Smith had said the *Carpathia* was on her way. Again she prayed, this time for a miracle.

"There are more men in the water!" the young boy cried. The seaman leaned over the side and grasped the jersey of a man clinging to the grabline. Slowly he hauled him aboard.

"She's done for," the rescued man spluttered, "She's shipping water too fast!"

Another man, pulled from the sea, pleaded frantically in French. Lucy's sensitive ears picked up his ranting. "He's afraid he's going to be thrown overboard and drown." She called to the crewman in charge.

"Don't we all, ma'am? Tell him he's got to row." His tone softened. "If you'd be so kind, ma'am?"

Lucy spoke quickly in French, and the man fell silent as another man was snatched from the water.

"Papa will be in another boat," Cecilly said, "probably with Colonel Astor. And Hardie and Marshall, of course."

"They'll be on one of the smaller boats," Lucy said. Although unconvinced by her own words, inwardly she clung to any small straw of hope. She shivered, hardly able to feel her toes in the bottom of the boat.

"She's going!" a terrified voice screeched. Both girls swung around and watched the ship, now low in the water, blazing light across the ocean.

"I can't look! All those people, why haven't they gotten to their boats?" Cecilly slumped forward, buried her head in her hands, and sobbed.

"They don't have any," Lucy answered under her breath, then prayed Cecilly hadn't heard.

"If I don't look, I can pretend it hasn't happened," Cecilly cried.

Lucy couldn't look away. She had to witness and remember. If she was to have any future, she knew she had to face this disaster squarely. She fixed her eyes on the ship. With the *Titanic* silhouetted against the sky, she made her final plea to the Almighty.

"Save him, please, God," she begged. "I know it's selfish of me, but spare him."

A low, deep groan reverberated across the sea followed by thunderous crashing sounds which grew louder and surrounded the small lifeboat. Suddenly the *Titanic's* lights went out, briefly flashed on again, and died. On the lifeboat, Lucy was surrounded by gasps and cries, many women burst into tears or stared blankly across the still waters.

Stranded in darkness, only the ship's silhouette remained bathed in moonlight. A single lamp flickered from her crow's nest.

"'Er bulkheads are going!" bellowed one of the rescued crewmen. To the sound of buckling steel, the ship's superstructure ripped apart and the great liner tilted, drowning her bow. Her stern rose clear of the water, exposing her giant propellers as she swung into a near vertical position. She remained there, motionless for a few moments, as swarms of human figures clung to her.

Lucy could hardly breathe. The thunderous noise grew louder. She imagined a wall of water surging into the ship's structure. The luxurious rooms she and the Grants had enjoyed so recently would be crushed. Stunned by the spectacle unfolding before her, she prayed for the many souls who clung to the aft deck and stern. Her heart went out to them. Their lives would be measured in minutes in the bitterly cold sea. A vicelike grip held her heart. Would Edwin or Sir Leyster be among them? She forced the thought out of her head, only to find it replaced with anger. Where was the rescue ship Captain Smith had promised them?

Emotions raw, she made herself endure the *Titanic's* last moments. Tears filled her eyes as she watched the ship's stern hang perpendicular in the water, motionless. How could such a disaster occur? Only a few hours ago they had enjoyed a concert given by the ship's orchestra.

"She's going!" a voice cried from the darkness.

It was true. Lucy watched the stern section settle back into the water, almost righting itself. Many people had jumped overboard. Anguished cries echoed across the ocean's surface as the stern rose again. Her giant propellers lifted high out of the water.

Along with other survivors in Boat Four, Lucy mouthed the Lord's Prayer as the Atlantic Ocean claimed the *Titanic*. The unsinkable ship slid beneath the black waters.

A murmur, "She's gone," drifted hauntingly around the open boat.

Her fingers numb, Lucy plunged her hand inside her dress and pulled out Edwin's watch. She caught the T-bar of the heavy chain in her crochet collar. Her hand shaking, she flicked open the gold case. But it was too dark to see the hands. She removed her leather gloves and managed to prise open the glass cover. She felt for the fingers— twenty minutes past two. Two large tears rolled down her cheeks.

She snapped the case shut, replaced the watch inside of her dress, and fumbled to get her hands back into her gloves.

"I...never thought it would...happen," Cecilly said.

Stunned by the ship's loss, the survivors gazed blankly as debris drifted on the surface. The water filled with people struggling for their lives. They splashed aimlessly, some trying to swim to the lifeboats, others clinging to whatever they could find, and hundreds floating in their white canvas life-preservers.

Aware of long, pale faces around her in the lifeboat, Lucy supposed they were all struggling to understand what they had witnessed. It was impossible to ignore the agonising screams of the people in the water. Voices pleaded, screamed, and wailed. Each cry squeezed her heart and filled her with guilt. Was Edwin amongst them?

"We're going back," the seaman in charge cried.

"No!" The terrified response came from survivors close to him at the stern.

"We'll be drowned too!"

"They're all lost," another voice said.

"What are you waiting for? We must save them!" other voices called from the darkness.

"There are people still alive out there. We've room in the boat. We can try to save a few." He pushed hard on the tiller to bring the boat about.

Although progress was slow, they rescued six men, all from the *Titanic's* crew—stewards, stokers, seamen. Their rank or profession mattered little as they were hauled on board.

"What's that sound?" Cecily grasped her cousin's hand. The dull thuds persisted.

From her seat at the edge of the lifeboat, Lucy saw dozens of bodies clad in their white cork jackets floating stiffly on the water's surface. She didn't tell Cecily they were colliding with dead bodies. "Nothing for us to worry about," she said.

Eventually, the desperate cries expired. But then Lucy found the silence more painful. When someone called for help, it meant they were still alive. Now the stillness grew eerie. She shivered at the realisation they were moving through a liquid graveyard.

A baby crying broke the deathly silence. Lucy squeezed her cousin's hand. "Life goes on, we must never give up."

"What happens now?" A male voice called from somewhere in the middle of the boat.

"We row in the direction of the rescue ship." The seaman held the tiller marking his authority.

"Aye, and where's that?"

Eyes, some swollen with tears, scanned the horizon for a light, a sign, or some signal.

"There's a light to starboard," one of the rescued men called.

Out of the darkness they sighted a dim light and began rowing towards it.

* * * *

"I'm so cold...so dreadfully cold," Cecilly sobbed. "My lovely nightgown, the one bought for my wedding night. It's gone."

"Think of Frank." Lucy put her arm around her cousin's shoulders. "He'll be frantic with worry when news of the disaster breaks in New York."

"Cecilly, stop crying at once." It was Lady Grant's voice.

Amazed, both girls turned towards her.

"I've told you to remain with Nanny Jones and no amount of weeping will change my mind. Grandmama is poorly. The sickroom is no place for a child."

"Yes, Mama." Cecilly turned to Lucy. "Oh, dear, Grandmama died years ago. Whatever shall be we do? Mama has lost her senses."

"Humour her," Lucy replied. "She's in shock. She'll be herself again soon."

Lucy swallowed and held back her grief. She clung to hope, however dim that hope might be. "Until I'm told otherwise," she mouthed to herself, "Edwin's alive."

* * * *

The night stretched on. Strained, tired eyes scanned the horizon for a rescue ship. As the minutes passed, few people spoke. Some women wept, and those who could took turns at the oars.

"I declare, it feels warmer when we're rowing," Cecilly whispered.

"I spoke to Captain Smith," Lucy told those around her. "He said the *Carpathia* was coming."

"Are we gaining on the light?" Cecilly asked.

"I don't know, but I think I heard someone say there was another."

The dim lights turned out to be some of the other lifeboats. They pulled alongside one of them. An officer from the other boat ordered the lifeboats to be tied together.

"Lucy! What was that?" Cecilly called after a long stretch of silence.

The shrill blast of whistle sounded again.

"Come over and pick us up!" a voice shouted across the water.

"Aye, aye, sir!"

Some distance away Lucy saw men huddled together, standing on water! However, as they neared the strange figures, she realised they stood back to back on the keel of an upturned boat. The eerie scene seemed ghostly, as if some of the

Titanic's lost souls had returned to haunt the living.

But they weren't ghosts, simply living beings in need of help. Female voices replied, asked for names, and pleaded for loved ones. Quickly Lucy glanced along the double rank of drenched survivors. Collars turned up, hats pulled down, each man had fought to stay alive in the bitter cold. *Could Edwin and Uncle Leyster be among them?* Her nerve snapped, and she looked away. If she didn't look, then she could keep her hopes alive a little longer.

* * * *

As dawn broke, a steamer was sighted on the horizon. Word spread that she was the promised *Carpathia*, four or five miles off. Ironically, floating ice surrounded them, as if to remind them what had caused the *Titanic's* demise. The survivors in the lifeboat flotilla rowed gallantly towards the rescue ship, heartened by her presence.

But the dawn also brought the wind and before long the sea became choppy. It splashed up over the gunwales into the bottom of the lifeboat. Nearly everyone in Boat Four found themselves up to their knees in water. Desperately people began to bail the water out of the boat with their hands or anything else they could find.

Gradually they pulled alongside the rescue ship. Lucy watched her fellow survivors as they gazed up at the rope ladders which had been strung out down the ship's sides. The women went up first, mounting the ladders with an extra rope looped around their shoulders.

When it was Lucy's turn she threw off her life-preserver and nearly discarded the leather satchel which Marshall had given her. She had pushed it up her back between her life-preserver and her coat when she had boarded the lifeboat. Hauntingly his words echoed in her ears: "My most valuable possession." She picked up the portfolio and secured its leather strap around her wrist. Slowly she climbed aboard the rescue ship. Crewmen hauled Lady Grant up in a bosun's chair.

"Brandy?" A steward offered them a small glass.

Lucy sipped the mellow liquor. Although it was foreign to her palate, she appreciated the warming effect when she drank it.

"This way, please, ladies." A crew member directed them. "There's coffee and sandwiches in the lounge for everyone."

They followed the column of survivors as directed and found Lady Grant a seat. "Stay with your mother," Lucy said to Cecilly. "I believe she needs the doctor. Miss Jenkins, Monique, do either of you require medical attention?" Both maids shook their heads. "I'm going to find the doctor for her ladyship. Stay here with Miss Grant and do not let anyone separate you."

Lucy didn't have to look far; he was on the far side of the large room, attending to a child. When he had finished he came to them.

"Lady Grant is in shock," he reported. "Get her hot, sweet tea and give her this sleeping draught."

He handed a small white packet to Lucy. Within a few minutes, they were led to a first-class cabin by one of the *Carpathia's* stewards.

"This is a lot smaller than our staterooms." Cecilly pulled a face. "Do we have to share?"

"It will be adequate for our needs," Lucy replied.

Working together, Miss Jenkins and Monique helped Lady Grant into bed. They gave her hot tea containing the sleeping draught the doctor had prescribed. Soon she drifted off to sleep.

"My boots are wet through." Cecilly held up her skirt. "My petticoat's damp, and look! My dress and coat are totally ruined by sea water."

"We'd best start drying them out," Lucy suggested, moving towards the stove.

A few moments later, after knocking on the door, two stewardesses entered. They carried a straw-filled mattress between them and placed it on the floor. "This is for the maids, Miss," the senior woman said, addressing Lucy.

"Do we all have to share?" Cecilly's tone was harsh.

"Yes, Miss. With so many new passengers coming on board, most of ours have doubled up. Everyone has been very understanding."

"Thank you for your help." Lucy said. "As we have our own maids, we should be able to manage by ourselves. We just need to sleep."

After the stewardesses left, Lucy and Cecilly removed their dresses and spread them around the cabin to dry. The two servants undressed and settled down on the straw mattress on the floor, whilst Lucy and Cecilly sat on the remaining bed.

"As soon as Papa arrives on board, he'll find accommodations for Mama."

Cecilly's naive flippancy tried Lucy's patience. Tiredness had etched away at her tolerance level. She stretched out her arms and placed her hands on her cousin's shoulders. She meant to shake some sense into her, but realised Cecilly needed her compassion, not her anger. "You must prepare yourself. We might be the only survivors. There weren't enough lifeboats for all the men." She rushed the last few words. It was the only way she could say them.

"No," Cecilly protested. Her hands flew to her face. "I don't believe you!" Her body went rigid then she began to shake uncontrollably.

Lucy tightened her grip on Cecilly and drew her close. "We won't know for certain until a roll call is made of all the survivors. It is possible people were picked up by another ship. Don't give up hope, not yet. Not until—" She choked up and sniffed back a few tears. "You must look to the future. You have Frank. He loves you."

"But I love Papa, too."

"And I love Edwin. We're engaged." The reality of what she had just confessed overwhelmed her. She broke down and wept. The cousins clung together in their mutual grief until fatigue overcame them and they fell asleep.

* * * *

Lucy woke with no idea what time it was, except that it was daylight. She pushed herself up on her elbows. Her neck and back ached, probably from the rowing and climbing in and out of the lifeboat. She sank back onto the pillow and rubbed her neck to relieve the tension.

After a few moments she sat up. Cecilly slept soundly beside her, as did Monique and Miss Jenkins on the straw mattress on the floor. Lady Grant snored in the other bed. She didn't want to wake them, but she felt eager for news. What had happened to her uncle and Edwin?

Without disturbing the others, she crept out of bed, slipped her dress over her head, and buttoned up the bodice. Next she looked around the cabin for her coat and found it hanging near the stove. Like her dress, the coat felt damp and was stained by sea water. Somehow she managed to squeeze her feet into her soggy boots. Quietly she closed the cabin door behind her and made her way to the lounge where they had first been received.

"Can I help you, Miss?" a steward asked.

"Is there a list of survivors?" Her voice came out as little more than a whisper.

"I don't know, Miss. Ask Mr. Hughes, the Chief Steward—he's in the dining room. But I do know all the *Titanic's* lifeboats have been accounted for. We've—" he broke off. "Are you all right, Miss?"

Lucy felt the colour drain from her face as she suppressed the taste of bile in her mouth. She looked up at him and wondered how many more times he would have to deliver the same message before the day was done. "Please show me the way to the dining room."

She followed him along a corridor, narrower than the *Titanic's*, and down a flight of stairs. They entered the dining room, now overcrowded with people, some sitting on the floor. Women sobbed, others sat in shocked silence wrapped in blankets, their faces stark. There were some male survivors, but they were few. Her empty stomach turned over and a sharp pain gripped her heart as she began to give up hope that Edwin was amongst them. Aboard the lifeboat there had been hope, however unrealistic, that Edwin lived. Safely aboard the *Carpathia* she had to face the prospect that she had lost him to the sea.

"That's the Chief Steward over there, Miss. Will you be all right now? Only I've got other duties."

"Yes, thank you." Hardly knowing how her legs supported her, she picked her way across the room between the sorrowful groups of people to join the queue waiting to speak to the Chief Steward.

"Lucy!" A voice called to her.

She caught her breath. Had her ears deceived her? Was she hallucinating? Did she have sufficient strength to look around? And if she did, what would she see? The man she loved, or his ghost?

Swallowing deeply, she summoned what remained of her courage and turned around. Slowly, her eyes fixed on his face. Dark eyes sunken with weariness, eyelids hooded, he stared at her. "Edwin, thank God you're alive!"

He swept her into his arms. His breath warmed her cheek as she felt the urgency of his lips pressed against hers. His kiss, the most precious she had ever known, released the pent up tension within her. Her legs crumbled beneath her, and her world went black.

Chapter Twelve

Lucy woke, blinked several times, and stared at the ceiling. This wasn't her room; this wasn't the *Titanic*.

She shuddered as memory of the silhouette of the ship's stern slipping beneath the ocean haunted her. She snapped her eyelids shut to block out the horror of it. That didn't work. She could still hear the screams of those unfortunates in the icy water. She forced her eyes open. Would she wake up every day plagued by the events of that night? Was that the price she would pay for surviving the ordeal?

Desperate for any distraction, she sat up and glanced quickly around the small cabin. She was in a narrow bunk, fully clothed. A desk, a washstand, and a cupboard lined the opposite wall. A set of oil skins hung from the hook on the back of the door. The place smelled of tobacco. Light came in through a small porthole. She stared into blank space and listened to the throb of the ship's engines. This wasn't the cabin she had been given with Lady Grant, Cecily, and the maids. Where was she?

Edwin?

Her heart swelled with joy. Her prayers had been answered. Somehow Edwin had been snatched from an icy grave. If he had survived, perhaps her uncle had too. Her hopes lifted. But was she deluding herself? Had it all been a dream? Had she really seen Edwin and kissed him?

"Edwin!" She called his name several times and felt his watch move between her breasts. Retrieving it, she flicked open the case. It had stopped at twenty minutes past two. Hot tears pricked her eyes. Covering her face with her hands, she tasted warm salty tears.

She cried until she could cry no more. Until everything she cared about paled into insignificance compared with her need to find Edwin again. She had to prove she wasn't hallucinating. She needed to be reunited with him, to hold his hand in hers, and to feel his lips upon hers once more.

Snapping the gold cased shut, she slipped it inside her bodice and pressed it against her heart. The watch was all she had of his, and she wanted to keep it close, forever. She dried her face with a corner of the bed sheet, threw off the blanket, and struggled to her feet.

There was nothing in the cabin to tell her where she was or to whom the cabin belonged. How long had she been away from the others? They would be worried about her. She wrenched open the door and stepped into the narrow corridor. A steward approached.

"Please help me, I'm from the *Titanic*. My name is Miss Mainwaring. Can you help me find my family?"

"Certainly, Miss Mainwaring. Were you travelling first-class?"

"Yes, I was with Lady Grant, Miss Grant, and two maidservants. We were taken to a cabin, but I have no idea where it was. Also, I'm looking for Lieutenant-Commander Hardie, have you seen him?"

"No, Miss, but I can find out which cabin you've been allocated. This way please, Miss."

She followed the steward into a crowded room, similar to the dining room but smaller. All the seats were occupied. People looked dazed, tired, and bewildered. Some had blankets around their shoulders, while others huddled together for comfort. But it was the sound of women weeping that touched her raw emotions. A few children ran around, oblivious to their plight, whilst the stewards in attendance looked exhausted. The scene could not have been more different from the relaxed atmosphere of the previous afternoon aboard the lost ship.

"If you'll wait here, Miss, I'll get your cabin number from the Purser."

As she watched him leave, she recognised a maidservant with a small boy. "Have you seen Lieutenant-Commander Hardie?" she asked her.

"No, Miss."

"Can I be of assistance?"

Lucy swung around at the sound of an American voice. For a brief moment her hopes lifted. Marshall? She caught her breath then let out a long sigh. The gentleman she had met on the Boat Deck minutes after they had struck the iceberg stood before her.

"Colonel Gracie, ma'am, at your service."

"We spoke on the Boat Deck, I remember, you told me to look after my family."

"I did indeed, ma'am, but I overheard you asking about Hardie. I have good news: he was rescued with me. We were with Second Officer Lightoller on an upturned boat and transferred to Boat Twelve. We were amongst the last survivors to come aboard."

"Oh, Colonel Gracie, you do not know how indebted I am to you. I did see Edwin, but I was so exhausted, I collapsed. When I awoke I was so confused I began to think my mind was playing tricks on me. Oh, thank you. But do you know where he is now?"

"Probably sleeping, ma'am. I believe he went with Lightoller when we boarded."

She looked at the dressing around his head. "Are you injured, Colonel?"

"Just a slight gash. We're the fortunate ones. It's now our duty to report our accounts to the world."

The steward returned. "Excuse me, Miss Mainwaring, I have your cabin number. If you would come this way?"

"Good-day, Colonel Gracie, and thank you very much."

* * * *

When she reached the cabin, a stewardess opened the door for her.

"Miss Lucy, would you care for some tea?" Monique held a cup out to her.

Lucy accepted it gratefully, "What time is it?"

"Nearly four o'clock," Cecilly said. Fully dressed, she had her back to the mirror. Her eyes were puffy and her complexion was covered in red blotches. "We were worried when we woke up and you were missing. Where have you been?"

"Searching for news about the rest of the survivors. I've seen Hardie; he's on board."

Cecilly's face lit up. "Oh, Lucy, thank God, and Papa?"

"No, he's still missing." Lucy couldn't bring herself to say all the *Titanic's* lifeboats had been recovered when there was still the slightest hope more survivors could be found.

Cecilly's face dropped. "My head hurts. I feel so miserable."

Lucy put her arm around her cousin's shoulders and drew her close. She glanced at her aunt, who was sitting up in bed, sipping tea. Although Lady Grant appeared outwardly calm at the news that her husband was still unaccounted for, her grey pallor worried Lucy. Several survivors in the dining room had a similar demeanour, and she feared her aunt might succumb to hysteria.

Miss Jenkins answered a firm knock on the door. "It's Dr. McGhee, my lady."

Lady Grant frowned. "I don't recall the name."

"He's the doctor who attended to us early this morning," Lucy explained.

"Of course," she nodded slowly. "Let him enter."

He strode into the cabin and placed his bag on the dressing table. "How are you feeling, ladies?" Both girls looked at Lady Grant.

"Given our burdens, we are managing." Lady Grant's speech was slow and her voice subdued. She placed her teacup on the bedside table. "Please convey my thanks to the captain and officers for their hospitality."

Lucy breathed a relieved sigh. Her aunt was speaking coherently and seemed to be aware of their situation.

Dr. McGhee nodded in reply to Lady Grant and glanced around the two berth cabin, now housing five. "I regret your accommodations are limited, but have you all been able to sleep?"

"Yes," Lucy and Cecilly said in unison. The two maids agreed.

"I am very tired. I haven't been able to sleep a wink since I boarded this ship," Lady Grant said. Her tone reminded Lucy of what her aunt had said about the *Titanic*. Lucy frowned and shook her head at the doctor.

"I will leave you another sleeping draught, but I must advise caution. The body and mind need time to come to terms with shock. Rest is recommended, which is provident as Captain Rostron has requested passengers keep to their cabins. Please ensure Lady Grant only takes a small amount, unless she is particularly restless. Excuse me, ladies, I have a number of other patients to see." Miss Jenkins held the door open for him as he left.

Soon afterwards they were disturbed by another caller. Lady Grant nodded her consent when Monique announced Lieutenant-Commander Hardie wished to speak to them.

Lucy's heart lurched, her breath shortened, and she bit her lips. Tension wound inside her like a coiling spring, yet she wanted nothing more than to see him again. When he entered the cabin, his unshaven face looked drawn. He removed his peaked cap and tucked it under his arm.

"Your call is appreciated. I know how difficult it is. Forgive me for not getting up, but I am excessively tired."

"If it is inconvenient, Lady Grant, I can return later."

Lucy didn't speak but noted the dark smudges under his eyes and the uneasiness in his manner. He raised his eyebrows to her slightly as he crossed the narrow confines of the cabin. It was the only sign of recognition he gave her.

"It's my responsibility to tell you what happened after you boarded the lifeboat. I hope my account will help you."

"Please take a seat," Lady Grant offered, indicating one of the chairs. He hesitated and looked at Lucy.

She smiled briefly back at him, then realised he was waiting for them to sit down before he took the chair. "Cecilly, come and sit beside me on the bed. Aunt Maud, do you want the servants to leave?"

"I prefer Jenkins and Monique to remain. They shared our terrible ordeal and have a right to hear what happened, especially if it involves the master and his valet. If you have no objection, Hardie?"

"Certainly not, your ladyship," he said and sat down. "Your lifeboat, Boat Four, I understand was the last to leave the ship Second Officer Lightoller told us there were two small emergency boats to get away. We—that's Sir Leyster, his valet, and myself—followed him to help with the loading. Once the main lifeboats had gone, the situation on board became desperate as people realised the gravity of their situation. The ship was sinking fast, with her bow awash. Panic broke out." He paused and took in a deep breath. "It was harrowing. Some men took it calmly, while others—"

"Were all the lifeboats launched?" Lady Grant asked.

"Yes, my lady. The situation worsened as the water rose, and crowds of people struggled to run along the deck as the ship listed. Sir Leyster said there was insufficient lifeboat capacity for the size of the ship, and the Board of Trade regulations fell short for modern shipping capacity. 'Parliament must legislate for adequate lifeboat space,' I recall him shouting."

"So typical of my husband to think of the politics."

"We heard Lightoller call for men to help uncover the two small boats, one on the deck and the other on the roof of the officers' quarters. We had a task; hopefully we could save a few more lives. I helped Lightoller uncover the first boat and heard Sir Leyster shout that the men were needed to free the second."

Lucy pressed her lips together, the throb of the *Carpathia's* engines humming in her ears. As she listened to Edwin's harrowing tale unfold, tension built up inside her. She looked down at her hands, drawn into tightly clenched fists. Slowly she uncurled them and rubbed the bright red marks where her nails had bitten into her palms.

"I helped adjust the davits to lower the first boat. They were the latest design, built to launch several boats apiece! I was furious when I saw them. There could have been enough boats for everyone."

"Did the men free both the boats?" Lady Grant asked.

"Only the first one. I helped man the davits, ready to lower the boat when it had been filled. They called for more women. When there appeared to be no more, a few men were allowed in and we lowered the boat into the water."

"Then Papa could have gone in the boat!" Cecily said.

"Yes, but he was on the roof of the officers' quarters helping to free the second boat. I climbed up there with Lightoller. He shouted at his crewmen to cut the ropes as the sea was rising around us. The oars were thrown out. Sir Leyster and I placed them against the wall of the officers' house. We hoped to break the fall when the boat was pushed from the roof. But she slipped and landed with a mighty crash on the Boat Deck. We thought she was done for..." He took a deep breath and looked at each of them in turn.

"The sea rose rapidly and washed over the Boat Deck. Our boat drifted off, keel up. Men were in the water, struggling to right her. People moved back to the stern as a large wave came crashing up to the bridge. I saw Captain Smith as he bellowed the master's final order: 'Every man for himself!' Sir Leyster offered me his hand. I took his in both of mine. 'We've got our orders,' he said. 'It's our duty to save our own lives now, God willing.'" He broke off, leaned forward, and buried his head in his hands.

Lady Grant gave Miss Jenkins a sharp look. "A cup of tea at once."

Hardie shifted on his chair, his head bowed. No one spoke. The rattle of a tea cup being held out to him broke the silence. He looked up, his dark eyes glassy, reached for the tea, and took a few sips.

Hot tears stung Lucy's eyes as her throat dried. She watched Edwin's jaw muscles twitch as he finished his tea.

"His last words were—" He broke off and looked directly at Lady Grant. "Do you wish me to continue?"

She nodded her approval.

"We could see perfectly. The ship's lights blazed almost to the end. The ship's bow was well down in the water, her forward compartments completely flooded. The sea was but a few feet away from us. Sir Leyster looked astern and shouted, 'There's still women aboard!'"

The cabin was silent, except for the incessant churn of the ship's engines. Hardie bowed his head and wiped beads of perspiration from his forehead with the back of his hand. He looked up.

"His last words, my lady, were not for himself, but concern for others. It was the last time I saw him."

Lady Grant sat motionless. Warm tears streamed down Lucy's cheeks. She let them fall. Only Cecilly broke the silence, letting out several painful cries. She turned to Lucy and collapsed into her arms, sobbing loudly.

After a few minutes, Hardie said, "To the end he never thought of himself, my lady. There wasn't time to launch the last boat. A large wave swept over the deck, and I believe it took Sir Leyster. I clung to the ship's rail but she was going fast. I had to abandon her. I know no more of Sir Leyster's fate."

No one spoke. Cecilly's sobs eventually subsided and Lady Grant said, "Thank you. It is a great comfort to know he acted bravely. But tell us what happened to you."

"The water was bitterly cold, far colder than I had ever imagined. I was in a whirlpool. The current swirled around me, pulling me down. The pressure on my ears was so enormous I thought my head would burst. With all my strength I swam under water as far away from the ship as I could. I held my breath until I couldn't stand it any longer, and I prayed."

Lucy's eyes roamed over his large frame. His shoulders were hunched over and his head hung low. Had he thought of her at that moment? It was too much to hope for. He'd been saved, wasn't that enough?

"Possessed of a second wind, I broke the surface and hit a piece of wreckage. I believe it was a small plank. I tucked it under my arm. Next I found a wooden crate and hung onto that for as long as I could." He looked up sharply. "I've been at sea many years. The chance of survival in icy waters is measured in minutes. If I wanted to live, I had to get out of the water. I looked at the ship, stern perpendicular to the horizon and watched as she slid beneath the ocean. The calm sea swallowed her so easily. A thin, smoky vapour, like mist, hung over the water. Wreckage lay strewn across the wreck site, and across the surface of the flat ocean, hundreds of screaming voices—"

"We heard them too," Cecilly blurted out, then plunged into another fit of weeping. Again Lucy comforted her.

"I clung to my wreckage and started to pass frozen bodies in the water. I became aware of an eerie silence surrounding me. People were no longer struggling or calling. I don't know how long I was in the water. It seemed an eternity. Then my salvation; I saw the boat we had spent our last efforts trying to launch some distance away. She was upturned with a dozen or so men balanced on her keel. I discarded my crate and struck out towards her. When I came alongside, I recognised Lightoller at her stern. He was using a piece of boarding as an improvised paddle. I called to him and scrambled aboard. Others followed as best they could. Exhausted, some lay across the boat, and others stood as I did. Perched on a knife-edge between life and death, we clung to each other until two of the other lifeboats came back to pick us up. One, I believe was yours, but I went in the other with Lightoller." He held his head back, eyes to the ceiling, a tortured expression on his face. "Why have I been spared when so many were lost?"

Desperately Lucy yearned to get close to him and hold him in her arms. Instead she hugged Cecily until her cousin's sobs subsided.

"We have all been spared." Lady Grant's voice was quietly serene. "We have been granted life, Hardie. It is not for us to ask why. Do you know what happened to Hobbs, my husband's valet?"

"He was at his master side to the end. I suppose he was taken by the same wave which swept us overboard. I didn't see him again."

Cecily looked up, her eyes swollen and red. "What happened to Mr. Marshall?"

Lady Grant gave her daughter a sharp look. Cecily burst into tears again and reclaimed Lucy's shoulder.

Hugging Cecily, Lucy watched Hardie slump back in his chair. His eyes narrowed at the mention of the man's name and a muscle twitched along his jawline. "He left us when you boarded the lifeboat. Afterwards I saw him talking to the band leader, probably to request a tune." He locked eyes with Lucy's. "That's the last I saw of him."

Lucy knew he must have witnessed Marshall's farewell. She swallowed, trying to rid herself of her guilt over the bold kiss the American had given her. Somehow she had to convince him that Marshall was nothing more than a friend. But this was not the moment; she needed to speak to Edwin alone.

"We have heard...rumours," Lady Grant said, "of a very serious nature that Captain Smith knew of the ice and did not slow down."

Hardie didn't reply immediately, and Lucy wondered what he was thinking. Eventually he spoke. "Loss of so many lives is bound to give rise to speculation. We want to know why. But until evidence is examined, speculation is all it can be. Lightoller is the senior surviving officer. He was last to come aboard this morning. I understand he was off duty when the incident occurred, but doubtless he will be giving evidence at the inquiry."

"Inquiry?" Lady Grant echoed.

"Most certainly there will be one, so do not give too much credence to idle gossip. I'm confident the official inquiry will discover who is culpable. There is little more I can add, except Captain Rostron expects to arrive in New York in a few days. If you will excuse me, Lady Grant, I will take my leave."

"Thank you, Hardie, you don't know how comforting your words have been."

Lucy didn't say anything, but gazed lovingly at him as he rose and made for the door. How she wanted to take him in her arms, comfort him, and love him.

* * * *

As the door closed behind him, Lucy sprang to her feet. "Aunt Maud, I must go after him. I've forgotten to return Ed—Hardie's pocket watch."

"Very well. Hurry, catch him before he disappears into the smoking room."

Lucy picked up her skirts and dashed outside into the corridor. At the corner at the main staircase, she turned. Where had he gone?

People stood everywhere—in the corridors, on the staircase. They stood around, their faces long, hardly speaking to each other. She picked her way between them and made for the doors to the deck. A blast of cold air hit her as she spied his familiar figure leaning over the ship's rail, alone, and gazing out to sea.

"Edwin?" She pulled the sleeve of his woollen jumper.

He turned to face her, his dark eyes distant.

"I've brought this back." Nervously she offered him the watch, but he made no move to accept it. "Please take it. I'm afraid it's stopped."

His eyes were a sea of confusion, a muscle twitched along his jawline. She searched his eyes, seeking some way of breaking down the barrier between them. "I'm sorry about the watch. I held it when the ship sank and opened the case. In the darkness, I felt for the fingers, but my clumsiness must have stopped the movement."

He glanced briefly at the watch in her hand, then at her. "Keep it."

"But it's yours, your grandfather's."

"It's no longer important to me."

"Am I still important to you?" When he didn't reply she said, "We're still going to be married, aren't we?"

"If that's what you want." The lines around his eyes deepened.

"Of course I want us to be man and wife," she sighed, "but if you have changed your mind—"

"I want our future to be together," he cut in, "but here, right now, it all seems so wrong to be talking of our future. We have been through so much. Can we leave matters unsaid until we hurt less inside?" He grabbed her upper arms and pulled her towards him. "Don't you understand, Lucy? There are plenty of tomorrows for us."

She hoped he would kiss her. She wanted him to kiss her. Instead, his arms dropped abruptly to his sides.

"Too many perished." He stared across the ocean, as if paying his final respects to them.

Lucy stood silently beside the man she loved for several long moments until she began to shiver. Would they ever be the same people again, or were they suffering the after-effects of shock? She didn't know, but her feelings hadn't changed. She wanted to be his wife more than ever.

Perhaps he was right, she conceded. The disaster would leave scars, especially emotional ones. They would not be immune. Tears welled inside her as she reached out to him. "I need you, Edwin."

"I know."

Chapter Thirteen

When Edwin left her at her door, she watched his tall figure stride down the corridor. When he was out of sight, she slipped the pocket watch down the front of her bodice between her breasts. She had kept it there throughout the rescue. It would stay there, she decided, next to her heart.

She knocked on the door and was surprised when Cecilly answered. Inside she found her aunt and cousin alone. "Where have the maids gone?"

"To dinner, apparently we have to eat according to a rota as there isn't enough room to seat everyone in the dining room. First-class dinner is at six-thirty." Cecilly said.

"I'm glad we are alone. Aunt Maud, Cecilly, I have promised to marry Lieutenant-Commander Hardie."

Cecilly took her hands in hers. "I'm so pleased for you, but I have melancholy in my heart for Papa. I'm sure you understand why I'm not jumping around with joy. I just don't feel like celebrating. I remember you told me earlier this morning, just before we went to sleep. That's why I was beginning to think I'd dreamt it."

"It's real, Cecilly and I know it's hard to feel happy about anything. Shock and grief have changed everyone."

"They have indeed," Lady Grant said, "but we must all be very brave. I am relieved that you are to be settled. Hardie is a good man. Sir Leyster thought very highly of him."

* * * *

The engagement wasn't discussed over the next few days. Although Lucy thought a great deal about it, she watched as almost everyone who had been rescued became enveloped in personal grief. The news that the *Carpathia* carried the only survivors spread like a plague. Nearly every woman aboard had lost either a husband or a father. Whole families had perished, especially those travelling third class.

Lucy attended several of the short memorial services. She found great comfort in them. But the one for the Irish emigrants moved her the most. Few had survived from third class. She closed her eyes and remembered the throng of young people she had watched embark at Queenstown. A cold shiver invaded the marrow bone of her arms and legs when she recalled those girls. Most likely they were the same ones Sir Leyster had seen being left aboard the sinking ship. Their journey to the New World had been short. She prayed they were safe in the world they had gone to.

Lucy saw little of Edwin. Although they ate in the first-class dining-room with the *Carpathia's* first-class passengers, he didn't join them there. There was so much she wanted to discuss with him, but the right moments didn't seem to occur.

She had told him about waking up in a small cabin, alone in part of the ship unknown to her.

"I carried you there," Edwin had said. "When you fainted, I couldn't leave you in the dining room, and no one knew your cabin number. So I took you to the one I'd been allocated. It was an officer's cabin, near the bridge. I intended to stay with you, but Captain Rostron wanted my report of the sinking first hand. I had to leave you. When I returned, you had gone. I met Colonel Gracie shortly afterwards and he told me you had returned to your cabin with your party. That's how I knew where to find you."

Captain Rostron visited the dining room on several occasions. He advised everyone to write reports of what they had seen on the night of the disaster. Lucy spent a considerable amount of time working on her personal account, but she didn't dare commit to paper what had happened to the Comte D'Every.

Glimpses of Marshall and the comte brawling in the stateroom flashed before her at odd moments. Marshall had assured her that the Belgian wasn't dead. But how could she be sure? They had left an unconscious man in a sinking ship. Wasn't that murder?

If the blow hadn't killed him, he could have made for a boat. She tried to cling to that narrow thread of hope. The man lived by his wits. Deception was second nature to him. But then she recalled his momentary look of incredulity. Like so many others, he probably hadn't considered the slightest possibility of the ship foundering. By why had he sought her out? What plans had he believed she had? She had unknowingly witnessed his part in espionage, but wasn't he known throughout Europe as a spy? Her head throbbed. There was so much she didn't understand.

On Wednesday afternoon, she sat in the cabin with the others. On her lap she had a notebook, given to her by one of the *Carpathia*'s original passengers. They had been generous, donating clothing, footwear, and writing materials to the survivors. Whenever she recalled a small incident or snippet of information, Lucy felt duty bound to record it. Her notebook contained descriptions of fellow passengers, snatches of conversation, and the important facts she had gleaned from her brief talks with Captain Smith and Mr. Andrews. She had just finished a sentence when the ship's siren blasted. Shocked, her heart pounded, her temperature rocketed, and she jumped to her feet.

"We're sinking!" Cecilly wailed, turning frantically this way and that in the confined space.

Lady Grant stood up, opened her arms to her daughter, and clenched her to her ample chest. "There's nothing to worry about. It's only fog. I've heard this ship's signal before. We'll slow down, but I've every confidence Captain Rostron will get us safely to New York."

Thankful for her aunt's calm reassurance, Lucy felt a huge weight lift from her. Lady Grant was more herself, opinionated and, at times, domineering, but she had been restored to them. Lucy doubted if their lives would ever be the same again. But knowing life must go on, she was determined to live hers to the full. Silently she vowed to place greater store in her aunt's intuition, especially as she had been wary of sailing on the *Titanic's* maiden voyage. Together they stood for a few silent moments, united by their experience, family connection, and love.

* * * *

The *Carpathia* entered New York harbour on the night of the 18ᵗʰ, surrounded by tugs. For Lucy it was a very different first view of America than the one she had anticipated. She stood on deck with Cecilly and Edwin as they slipped past the Statue of Liberty, which was silhouetted against the night sky. Like the majority of the *Carpathia's* passengers, they were anxious to reach land.

"Look, the decks are crowded with people." Lucy pointed to the armada of tugs approaching.

"They're reporters," Edwin said. The little boats came closer, and a chorus of shouting through loud hailers bombarded the ship. "Are they completely insensitive?"

As the *Caparthia* edged her way to the vacant White Star piers thousands of people crowded along the waterfront. "Why are all these people here?" Cecilly asked "How will Frank find me?"

"They're sightseers," Edwin replied. "News travels fast. But don't worry, Miss Grant, we will find Mr. Johnson when we have been through U.S. immigration."

Lucy clung to Edwin's arm, taking comfort in his strength beside her. She watched as the

Titanic's empty lifeboats were lowered into the water which should have been occupied by the mother ship. "What are they doing with the lifeboats?"

"Returning White Star's property," Edwin said.

It took some while until the *Carpathia* edged her way alongside the Cunard pier. Both girls gasped as an enormous explosion of light illuminated the ship. "What was that?" Lucy asked.

"Press photographers anxious to get pictures," Edwin replied.

Finally, they tied up and gangways were pushed across to the *Carpathia's* decks. They had arrived in America.

"I do hope Frank is here," Cecilly said for the umpteenth time, "because I'm never going to set foot aboard a ship again. I swear it!"

Lucy eyed her speculatively. "Best not make any rash promises."

Cecilly sighed. "I hope I like America, because I don't know what I shall do if I don't."

* * * *

Throughout the final part of their voyage to New York, Lucy hadn't seen as much of Edwin as she would have liked, and when she did see him it was usually in the company of others. But not once had he said he loved her. If only she could get closer to his thoughts and feelings. There was so much to be discussed about their future together, their mutual hopes and ambitions. But he had shut her out.

When disembarkation began, a slow, snakelike procession of mainly female survivors, wended its way down the gangway. People were anxious to leave the sea behind them, but few hurried. They were weary and grief-stricken. But for some, during the last two days of the voyage grief had turned into anger and blame. Men who had survived were treated with contempt by those whose loved ones had sacrificed themselves. The atmosphere had become highly charged. Male survivors were accused of cowardice and were increasingly regarded as dishonourable.

When it was the Grant ladies' turn to be conducted down the gangway to the quayside, Edwin accompanied them. Gladness filled Lucy's heart when she felt dry land beneath her feet. They were shown to the quayside where a large space had been made to accommodate waiting automobiles. A man jumped out of one of the vehicles and rushed towards them.

"Frank!" Cecilly broke away from their party and hurried towards him.

He called her name and swept her off her feet. Locked together, he twirled her around.

"Cecilly," her mother snapped, "this is a public place. Remember you're British!"

Lucy smiled at her aunt's chastisement and felt sure Cecilly didn't hear a word. She was too wrapped up in Frank. And who could blame her? Cecilly always demonstrated her affection, and she had every right to be ecstatic. Had it not been for fortune, Frank would have sailed with them from Southampton, not Marshall.

Frank put Cecily down, apologised profusely for his exuberance, and conducted them to the limousine he had waiting. "My father and mother would consider it the greatest honour if you would accept their hospitality."

Lady Grant nodded. "Most kind."

Just as they were leaving, Edwin stepped forward. "I have to report to the British Embassy in Washington." He turned to Lady Grant. "Please permit me to call upon you within the next few days."

Again she nodded her approval of the arrangement and stepped inside the vehicle with Cecily.

The gentlemen shook hands. "We've had a real anxious time, Hardie. You don't know how difficult it has been here. The news has been so confusing."

"You're aware Sir Leyster and his valet, Hobbs, were lost?"

Frank nodded. "I expected so when news came through that so many were missing."

"And your friend Marshall, too?"

"Really? I had no idea he was sailing with you."

"But didn't you give him your ticket?" Hardie asked.

"No, I transferred my passage to an earlier ship. I despaired about booking those tickets when I heard about the disaster. I began to wonder if Cecily would ever speak to me again."

"You couldn't have foretold the tragedy, Mr. Johnson," Lucy said.

"That's kind of you to say so, Miss Mainwaring. There'll be a lot of questions asked and a great deal of soul-searching done before the *Titanic* is allowed to rest." He held the door of the automobile open for her.

Before getting in, she drew Edwin to one side. "If Marshall didn't travel on Frank's ticket, how did he fund the crossing?"

"I don't know."

She gazed up into his eyes. "When will I see you again?"

"Early next week I'll call at the Johnsons."

* * * *

On Monday, four days after disembarkation, Edwin called at the Johnson mansion. He was received by Mrs. Johnson, Lady Grant, Cecilly, and Lucy. As they were in mourning, the ladies wouldn't normally have received visitors, but an exception was made for him, due to the unofficial engagement. Lucy disliked wearing black and felt very dour when he was announced.

He entered the drawing room, strikingly handsome in his dark uniform, a black armband his only indication of bereavement. As soon as she saw him, Lucy longed to reach out to him, touch his hand, and feel his warm breath on her face. Shamelessly she yearned for the intimacy of the conservatory. But in the Johnson household, she could only smile, make polite conversation, and hope for a few private words with him later.

"How long will you be in New York?" Mrs. Johnson asked.

"Until the end of the week; afterwards the inquiry moves to Washington. Unfortunately, I've no idea when I shall be needed," he said.

Hearing he would be in town for a few days raised Lucy's hopes of them spending some time together. His face was less drawn than the last time she had seen him, and she hoped she too looked in better health, although black made her look pale.

When Edwin requested a brief interview in private with Lady Grant, Lucy hoped he had come to offer for her formally. The possibility of announcing the engagement publically lifted her spirits.

"Use the library, Lady Grant; you won't be disturbed there," Mrs. Johnson said.

After they left, Cecilly said, "Lucy is on the verge of matrimony, too. I do believe Hardie is asking mother's permission now."

"I hope you'll be very happy," Mrs. Johnson said in a soft drawl. "Lieutenant-Commander Hardie is a very distinguished looking officer."

"Thank you, Mrs. Johnson. However, my father will also have to be consulted before I can marry. He is a minister and will want to conduct the ceremony himself."

"Oh, Lucy, I'd love you to stay here with us," Cecilly said.

"That is very kind of you, but I've been reading the American newspapers. If similar reports about the *Titanic* are being made at home, my father will be greatly troubled and want me back as soon as possible."

"What a pity, my dear, just as we were getting to know you. We shall miss you."

"Thank you, Mrs. Johnson, you have all been very kind," Lucy said.

They continued chatting until Edwin returned alone. He gave his apologies and asked Lucy to go to Lady Grant immediately. She blushed as he took her elbow and guided her through the open door into the hall.

"When can I see you alone?" she asked in a hushed whisper.

"Speak to your aunt first—she has news from you father."

Lucy placed her hand on the gold braid of his sleeve. "There's so much I want us to talk about."

"We've got the rest of our lives, haven't we?"

"Edwin, please be honest with me. If you have changed your mind, please say so. Don't marry me out of obligation. I know about your sense of duty, remember?"

He lifted her hand to his mouth and answered her with a soft kiss. "I haven't changed my mind," he whispered and kissed her cheek before leaving.

* * * *

"Lucy, are you listening?" Lady Grant held a Marconigram in her hand.

With the memory of Edwin's two kisses spinning in her head, Lucy hadn't been paying attention to her aunt. "I'm sorry, Aunt Maud, but it's been four days since I've seen Edwin, and he's quite taken my breath away."

Lady Grant let out a sigh. She waved the thin sheet of paper in the air. "This has arrived from your father."

The cost of a Marconigram must have bitten deeply into her father's purse. Lucy lifted her chin. "His message must be urgent. What does he say?"

"He wants—" Lady Grant corrected herself, "no, *demands* your immediate return. Doesn't he realise the anguish we have all suffered? Whatever is being said in London is no excuse for insensitivity. I quote, 'Hold Sir Leyster responsible for Lucy's welfare. Return her immediately.' How dare he take such a cursory tone with me?" She paced the room then with a deep sigh sank onto a sofa.

"Papa gets carried away sometimes. I'm sure he didn't mean to cause offence."

Lady Grant snorted her disapproval then patted the seat beside her. When Lucy sat down, she continued. "He has never been an easy person. Your dear mother was an angel, but he would try the patience of a saint!"

"I'm sorry, truly I am, but we don't know what is being said at home. Papa—"

"There's no need to apologise for your father's shortcomings. Fortunately you are nothing like him. Besides, we have more important matters to discuss."

Lucy breathed a sigh of relief as she listened intently.

"Hardie has made you an offer, though I understand the matter was decided rather hastily on board the ship. I remember we spoke briefly about it, however, nothing was settled. He thinks you may have second thoughts, is this so?"

"I—"

"You'd be foolish to turn him down," she cut in. "You are without a substantial dowry. You can't afford to let him slip through your fingers. As a second son, there's little chance of the title, but take my advice, my dear, accept him."

"But—"

"I know your mother would have approved of the match. She was such a gentle person."

"I—"

"And men like Hardie rarely propose more than once. Fix him now and ensure your father gives his permission without delay."

"I love Edwin, and nothing would give me greater pleasure than to be his wife."

"Oh!" Lady Grant stared at her for a few moments. "Yes, good. Write to your father immediately and to Hardie. A proposal is best accepted in writing."

"I shall do so at once." She wanted to shout her joy to the world, but did not think her aunt would appreciate her exuberance.

"Do you want to return home as your father dictates?"

"Perhaps it is for the best, but what is your advice, Aunt Maud?"

"Cecilly and I shall remain here. I have no mood for London at present. Doubtless the Admiralty will order Hardie back to England as soon as this American investigation is complete. Personally, I do not understand why the

Americans are concerning themselves with a wholly British matter. I'm informed there will be a proper British Inquiry in London as soon as the crew are released. My advice is simple. Accept Hardie, return home to your father, and prepare for your wedding."

Lady Grant made it sound so straightforward, but it wasn't. There remained one nagging doubt in Lucy's mind. She intended to marry Edwin, for better or worse because she loved him. If only he would say he loved her.

Chapter Fourteen

When Edwin called again the next morning Lucy was playing the piano in the drawing room for Lady Grant. Cecilly and Frank had gone out shopping, and Mrs. Johnson was sitting with her husband, who although over the worst of his recent illness, was confined to his bed.

Lady Grant rose when he was announced and offered him her hand. He crossed the room to greet her.

"Good morning, Hardie," Lady Grant said.

Lucy, who had stopped playing, also joined them. He looked so handsome in his dark uniform and crisp white linen. Her stomach clenched in anticipation of spending some time in his company.

"I'm so pleased to see you again," she said.

Lady Grant glanced quickly between the two of them. "That sonata was very soothing, Lucy, you should play more often. If you will excuse me, I have some letters to write. I'm sure you won't miss my company for half an hour, will you?"

"I could kiss your aunt for allowing us a few moments privacy," Edwin said as soon as the door had closed behind Lady Grant. He took Lucy in his arms and kissed her passionately.

Overwhelmed by his display of affection, she allowed her body to curve into his. Were her doubts about his feelings about to be conquered forever? Caressing the nape of his neck, she clung to him, returning his embrace.

His mouth parted gently, releasing hers. He dropped kisses along her jawline and claimed her lips again.

Held captive in his arms, she delighted in his strong body pressing against hers. She felt she was floating through the air because today she was his. Slowly she opened her eyes, in readiness to hear his declaration of love. But he remained silent. His hands slipped to her upper arms, and he stepped away from her. She wanted to stay close to him. Disappointed, she pressed her hands flat against his chest. "What's wrong?"

"Nothing."

"You never said anything about those final minutes when I boarded the lifeboat, but I feel I must speak about it. I must explain about Marshall." She felt his grip tighten around her upper arms when she spoke his name. "I liked him. I'd be lying if I denied my fondness for him as a friend. But friendship was all I ever felt on my part. I believe he was fond of me, but, Edwin, I swear, I never encouraged him."

"I know." He caressed her hair.

"Can you forgive me?"

"Forgive you? What is there to forgive?"

* * * *

The following afternoon, it was warm enough to sit outside. Cecily and Lucy took advantage of the spring weather by walking in the garden. As they strolled arm in arm, Cecilly said, "Frank showed me some sketches yesterday. Apparently Marshall had done them. I can't think how or when he did them, as he only came to Grosvenor Place a few times. They are rather good. Frank says he's going to have them framed for our new house."

A picture of Marshall leapt into Lucy's head. Initially, she remembered his lithe figure, but when she focused on his round face a pair of brilliant blue eyes flashed back at her. She shuddered. She couldn't explain what she was feeling. Perhaps her reaction had something to do with the leather satchel he had thrust into her hands? She nearly told Cecilly, but dismissed the idea. One day she would look at his sketches. When she felt stronger emotionally, she would be able to view them with fresh eyes.

"Look who's walking across the lawn," Cecilly said.

Lucy's heart skipped, as it did almost every time she saw Edwin.

Cecilly tapped her cousin's arm. "Now I can chaperone you."

The both giggled. It was the first time they had laughed together since the disaster.

Edwin fell into step with them. "It gladdens me to see you both in better spirits. What's the joke?"

"Oh, something quite silly," Cecilly admitted. "Me as a chaperone! Now I don't want to see any improper behaviour. I know you're engaged, but it is still unofficial. Remember the proprieties at all times." She waved a finger at them and laughed.

Lucy and Edwin looked at each other and laughed, too.

"Oh, no!" Cecilly cried. "I've just remembered, Mrs. Johnson asked me to pick flowers for the dinner table. By the way, Mama and Mrs. Johnson have gone to the dressmakers to order more gowns."

"How unexpected," Lucy said as she watched Cecilly disappear into the flower garden. Edwin took her hand in his, kissed her gently on the cheek, and together they ambled along the path.

When they reached a small arbour, Lucy turned to face him. "Cecilly mentioned Marshall a few minutes ago, and I recalled something odd about him. I was back at Grosvenor Place on the night of the theft, tip-toeing down the stairs. I saw a dark shadow, wearing a tight-fitting hood, like the ones aviators wear. God forgive me," she blurted out, "it was Marshall that night, I'd swear it!"

Edwin wrapped his arms around her and hugged her tightly.

"You warned me about him, but I was too full of myself. I knew you didn't like him, but I thought you were jealous."

"I was worse than that, I was furious."

She looked hopefully into his eyes. "Can you forgive me?"

"For what?"

"Not trusting your judgement, refusing to take heed of your warnings, disregarding your advice, and that's just for starters."

"You needed to find your own way."

She nestled her head against his shoulder, where she felt safe. After a few moments she asked, "What part did Sir Leyster's play in all this?" When he didn't reply, she lifted her head up. "Why were those documents in the safe that night? If they were so secret, why did my uncle have them?"

"He held a very special government post. He gathered information vital to the defence of our country."

"He was a spymaster?"

"No, he used agents, loyal patriots. We live in challenging times. The warmongers are working hard. Europe is rearming, and Britannia must do everything she can to retain naval supremacy. Foolishly, I exposed you to danger that night at the ball. I didn't know then that the Comte D'Every was behind the theft at the embassy. He twisted my impetuous plan about pretending we were lovers to his advantage. He spread the malicious rumours about us, implying I had compromised you that night in the conservatory. I had to protect you the only way I knew, by offering you marriage."

"And I turned you down."

"Sir Leyster told me, 'You'll have to do better than that if you're going to convince Lucy to be your wife.' And he was right, wasn't he? I made a mess of it. And the irony was, if only I'd seen what was so clear to him. I fell in love with you, Lucy, the first moment I saw you." He placed his hand under her chin, gently lifted her head up and gazed deeply into her eyes.

"And you are the only one I have ever loved, Edwin. I love you and you alone."

His eyes widened as he drew her towards him. He kissed her brow, her temples, and finally plundered the softness of her mouth.

In response, Lucy returned his kisses with renewed vigour. There was joy in her heart, and hope for their future. Suddenly she broke away from him. "Oh, Edwin! The satchel!"

"What?"

"The satchel. 'My most valuable possession,' that's what he called it. Do you remember? he rushed forward at the lifeboat, handed it to me, and kissed me."

"I saw him do that, but don't remember anything else."

"It contained the sketches he'd done on board. I never thought to look inside. I'd forgotten all about them until Cecilly reminded me earlier. I'll fetch it."

Lucy dashed back into the house. Edwin followed and waited at the bottom of the stairs for her.

Clutching the satchel, she raced back downstairs and pointed to the library. "Let's go in here."

Unbuckling the leather strap, she removed several sketch books. She flicked through them. Beautiful women smiled back at her from almost every page. There were quick sketches, pastels, cartoons, side notes outlining times and dates, and more recent sketches done on the *Titanic.* All were well executed, but none were so vibrant as the likenesses of herself.

"He's flattered me, drawn the woman he wanted to see."

Edwin glanced at several of the drawings. "Nonsense, you're beautiful. No wonder he wanted to sketch you, but there's no doubt the man had talent."

"Look at this, a self-portrait. It's only half-finished, but already he's captured the bright eyes and cavalier smile." She gazed at the pastel for several moments. It was hard to reconcile the amiable fellow in the picture with the thief who had plundered Sir Leyster's safe and stolen state secrets.

She searched the leather case again, digging deeply into the inside pockets, where her fingertips touched the edge of some paper. Turning the soft case almost inside out, carefully she extracted several thin sheets of almost transparent blue paper covered with a complicated series of diagrams. Her heart pounded. "Are these the plans he stole that night?"

Edwin replied by pointing to the Admiralty insignia in the corner. A relieved smile spread across his face. "These plans are highly confidential. I'm not allowed to tell even you, my darling, what they are for. His Majesty's Government and the Admiralty will be very grateful for their safe return."

"Why did he steal them?"

Refolded, Edwin put the plans into his pocket. "By the time we boarded the *Titanic*, Sir Leyster and I knew Marshall was an agent. We did not expect him to be sailing with us. You can imagine our surprise when he turned up claiming to hold Johnson's ticket. Although, as you know, Frank didn't give it to him."

"Why? What motivated him? Money? He wanted finance for his flying."

"I believe flying was only part of his game." Edwin paused, as if he was unsure of what or how much he wanted to impart to her.

"Do you think he realised the value of the plans?"

"Most definitely. Marshall knew exactly what he was doing."

"He was leaving Europe. Why? Did he intend to sell the plans in America?"

"Until two days ago, I probably would have come to the same conclusion. When I went to our embassy in Washington I learned that William Marshall was an agent of the United States. It was his job to steal those plans on behalf of his government. His cover story worked very well. We all believed he was a fortune-hunter and philanderer. In essence, he was patriot, although on British soil he would have been arrested as a common thief."

"So why did he give the stolen plans to me?"

He shrugged. "We'll never know. Perhaps he wanted you to have the sketches."

"Oh, Edwin, now I understand about the comte. He wasn't after us, was he? He came after Marshall. And now they are both gone."

"Keep the sketches, but the plans must be returned to the Admiralty immediately."

"Oh, dear, does that mean I shall be losing you?" She touched his arm, the gold braid on his sleeve felt rough.

"These plans are vital to naval warfare. However, knowing they have not been in foreign hands will be a great relief to those in command. And all thanks to you, my dear Lucy. However, I think you had better come with me and explain to the Admiralty lords how you came by such important information."

"But, the Admiralty's in London and—"

"Then there's no time to lose. We must leave on the next available ship. But before we leave, there is something."

"What?"

"I love you, Lucy Mainwaring. I've loved you from the first moment I set eyes on you reading the newspaper. So how do people get married quickly in this town?"

Lucy threw her arms around his neck and kissed him. Any worries she may have harboured about explaining herself to the Admiralty faded. She was in the arms of the man she loved.

Epilogue

Brilliant sunshine greeted the congregation as they emerged from Lichfield Cathedral. The memorial service over, the procession wended its way out of the Cathedral Close and formed up in the Museum Grounds, where a large statue swathed in sheets stood ready for the official unveiling.

Lucy put her gloved hands together to applaud the speech, but she couldn't clap. Her thoughts were far away in the mid-Atlantic. Her memory of that night was still very vivid. If she closed her eyes, she could feel the cold and hear the cries of the dying.

A young girl stepped forward and pulled the rope, revealing the larger-than-life bronze statue of her father, Captain Edward J. Smith. Lucy looked up at his stern features, full beard, commander's uniform, and cap and wondered what he would have thought of the gathered assembly. She recalled his words to her, the reassurance that a rescue ship was on its way and how he gave her his final salute. The *Carpathia* came, but too late to save the majority of lives on board the *Titanic*. She hoped he was at rest in his watery grave, for he was certainly not alone.

Discreetly she placed her gloved hand on her stomach and felt the movement of her second child. For a brief moment, she wished Edwin was with her, but he had returned to sea to command a war ship. Ugly rumours abounded throughout Europe about mobilisation and war.

Life had marched on for Lucy since the *Titanic's* ill-fated maiden voyage. She had married Edwin in New York and their first child, a son, had been born in the middle of April, very close to the first anniversary of the sinking. He had been christened Richard Leyster.

Cecilly and Frank were married in the summer of 1912. The wedding had been a grand affair, attended by the cream of New York society, according to the newspapers. But Lucy, already pregnant, hadn't been present. She regretted not seeing her cousin wed. However, the marriage had been blessed; Cecilly had a daughter and was expecting another child before the end of the year. Although Cecilly had settled in America, the cousins remained friends and corresponded regularly. But they were unlikely to meet unless Lucy crossed the Atlantic, because Cecilly refused to go to sea ever again.

Two minutes of silent vigil began. During the stillness, Lucy searched her heart. She had endured and survived a terrible tragedy, the memory of which always filled her with great sadness. She tried to be brave, as images and voices of the lost souls crowded her thoughts, led by her Uncle Leyster and William Marshall.

She couldn't stop tears rolling down her face as she relived the moment the *Titanic* slipped beneath the ocean and disappeared from all but human memory.

The End

About the Author

Lynda Dunwell is a LSE graduate and has taught economics and business studies for 20 years. She has worked as a press officer, advertisement copy writer and tourist information officer.

She is a member of the UK Romantic Novelists' Association and is an avid reader of historical romance. Her interest in the *Titanic* began as a child when she saw the film *A Night to Remember* and pestered her local library to get her a copy of the book of the same title by Walter Lord. Her fascination with the ship and the Edwardian era has never waned.

Lynda is a keen student of genealogy and has traced her paternal family line back to 1485. Currently she is researching her female line which she describes as "far more challenging."

Although based in the landlocked English Midlands, Lynda loves the sea and spends most of her vacations aboard cruise ships.

Website: http://www.lyndadunwell.com

Other Books by Lynda Dunwell

Regency Romances

Marrying the Admiral's Daughter

Captain Westwood's Inheritance

Colonel Weston's Wedding

Lady Mary's Elopement

Short Story Collections:

Titanic Twelve Tales

Fairy Tales Refocussed

All books available in paperback and ebook
format from Amazon